C000163976

FRAGMENTS OF YOUTH

FRAGMENTS OF YOUTH

RICHARD WILLIAMS

The Book Guild Ltd

First published in Great Britain in 2022 by
The Book Guild Ltd
Unit E2 Airfield Business Park,
Harrison Road, Market Harborough,
Leicestershire. LE16 7UL
Tel: 0116 2792299
www.bookguild.co.uk
Email: info@bookguild.co.uk
Twitter: @bookguild

Copyright © 2022 Richard Williams

The right of Richard Williams to be identified as the author of this
work has been asserted by them in accordance with the
Copyright, Design and Patents Act 1988.

All rights reserved. No part of this publication may be
reproduced, transmitted, or stored in a retrieval system, in any form or by any means,
without permission in writing from the publisher, nor be otherwise circulated in
any form of binding or cover other than that in which it is published and without
a similar condition being imposed on the subsequent purchaser.

This work is entirely fictitious and bears no resemblance to any persons living or dead.

Typeset in 11pt Minion Pro

Printed and bound in Great Britain by CMP UK

ISBN 978 1915352 415

British Library Cataloguing in Publication Data.
A catalogue record for this book is available from the British Library.

To my friends, family,
and those I've made music with
over the years.

CHAPTER 1

June 1997

Will looked up at the lights, relaxed his focus and let them blur into two blobs of colour and then merge, like an arty shot in a low-budget movie. He strummed away on his mint-green Telecaster and snapped back into the present; he had some backing vocals coming up.

'*Feels like I'm waiting for nothing,*' he chimed. *Was that in tune? Close enough.*

He looked down at his shoes, white with a fashionable amount of scuff, and out at the audience – all twelve of them. Between them and the stage was a kind of no man's land, where no one dared to tread. *One day people will get down early to our gigs and sit through the support bands to get those spots.* He smiled wryly to himself. He was on autopilot now, so consciously locked himself back in with the bass and kick drum as the song stuttered to an end; ringing out the final chord with conviction.

Applause.

It was the kind of applause heard at the local bowls club when a particularly delicate shot is played, but it was applause nonetheless.

He squatted down, unsteady on his haunches, and cranked the gain knob on his distortion pedal as far right as it would go. He lifted his guitar off and let it fall towards the floor, catching the strap just before it hit the ground – letting it drop enough to give the impression that he was *rock 'n' roll*, but being careful not to damage what was a birthday and Christmas present combined. Waves of feedback wafted across the venue. He raised one self-conscious hand to the audience and shuffled off the stage.

'We've been SharpShooter, thank you – goodnight!' bellowed Jake over the squall of noise, as if he were trying to reach the concessions stands at the back of Alexandra Palace.

The apathetic soundman failed to cut in with the house music, leaving the amp to squeal at the room. Will crawled tentatively back on stage and pressed down his distortion pedal with the palm of his hand to make it stop.

'Bloody soundman's fallen asleep,' he muttered, the knees of his jeans now covered in thick white dust from the stage.

'Great show, lads,' buzzed Jake.

'You think so?' asked Will.

'Yeah, we fucking stormed it.'

Will wiped a fresh bead of sweat from his forehead with the back of his hand. 'I think we sped up a bit on the last one.'

'There aren't many people,' said Luke, clumsily twirling a drumstick in his right hand.

'Who cares? You can only impress what's in front of you.'

'Well, we've impressed ten people, then.' Pete smirked, trying to cram his bass back into a case that was falling apart at the seams.

'Fuck 'em,' said Jake. 'It's a Tuesday night, out of town. The ghost of Elvis could wander on stage and these losers wouldn't look up from their pints.'

Will exhaled slowly. 'I just thought we'd be pulling more people by now.'

'Pulling more birds, you mean?' Jake laughed. 'Be patient, it's only been a year, and it took us six months to get our sound together.'

'Learn to play in time, more like.' Luke smiled.

'Yes – *the sound* of a band playing in time,' said Jake, grinning.

The gang had settled on the name SharpShooter because it was the only option that none of the band actively hated or threatened to quit over. It was the name of a wrestling move, the finisher of Bret the Hitman Hart, but it also had connotations of the Wild West, Jake would say, as if practising for a fanzine interview that was yet to come.

'Right – let's get pissed!' Jake cried, with forced revelry.

Will stuffed his battered FX pedals into the front pocket of his guitar case. 'We should load the gear first.'

Jake rolled his eyes theatrically but knew it was the right thing to do. They didn't want a repeat of the time at Malford Social Club when they got wasted on the generous rider of Carling and left half their stuff behind, calling up the next day to find it had been nabbed by some locals with a Cash Converters loyalty card.

Will pushed open the rickety fire exit and propped his amp against it to keep it open. It was the start of the summer and the fading light was holding on as they hobbled the gear into the car park and wedged it into the back of Pete's Vauxhall Corsa. He was the first one of the band to pass his test so had become designated driver by default – a role he pretended to dislike more than he actually did.

Back in the venue, the house lights dimmed and the gang watched from the wings as the next band took to the stage. Having long exhausted the twelve-pack of beers and multipack of Hula Hoops in the backroom, they decided to head to the bar.

'One, two, three, four!' screamed the drummer, standing up from his stool and flopping back down again as the band kicked into a dirgy riff.

The guys stopped short of the bar to watch for a few seconds before unanimously deciding they were crap. The singer had long hair and the bass player had his shirt off – both big red flags, they agreed.

'What you having, boys?' asked Jake. He'd recently started working on his dad's building site at the weekends so was a little flusher than the others – a position he clearly enjoyed. He was also the first of them to turn eighteen, meaning he no longer had to rely on his questionable fake ID to get served.

Will sidled up next to him and leant against the bar, the SharpShooter flyers they'd lovingly cut out at home now soggily stuck to it.

Jake ordered four pints from the barmaid, her dark roots sprouting through dyed blonde hair and her thick white makeup battling burgeoning crow's feet. He took

4

them from her with a wink, the plastic glasses squishing in his hands.

'I reckon I'm in there,' said Jake, turning to Will.

'Yeah, right.'

'Didn't you see the way she looked at me?'

'She was serving you – pretty difficult to do without looking at you.'

'Just you wait.' Jake winked.

The boys huddled together and watched the other band thrash through their set, the thunderous beat pulsating through the floorboards. Jake made another trip to the bar, the others trying hard not to make snide remarks as Hair screamed stuff like 'You're poison to me,' and 'Cut me deep and I'd bleed for you,' while Shirtless slapped the bass with his thumb, gurning as though the music were possessing him.

As last orders were called, they picked up their meagre fee from the promoter and meandered to the exit.

'One sec, boys, think I've left my tambourine,' said Jake, turning back.

Pete looked at the others. 'That's bullshit. His tambourine's in the boot.'

The trio leant lazily against the outside wall, their long shadows settling on the cracked pavement, and watched the remaining punters filter out of the venue.

'Who's skinning up, then?' asked Luke.

'Do it yourself. I've gotta drive,' Pete retorted.

Luke pulled out some Rizlas from his inside pocket and began to roll on the window ledge, a slight breeze making it difficult but not impossible. They passed around the joint, drawing on it slowly and puffing out little grey clouds of smoke.

Fifteen minutes or so later, Jake re-emerged, his jet-black hair clearly dishevelled and his belt missing a loop.

'Take your time,' said Pete.

'Sorry, it was the barmaid. Wanted me to meet her out back by the wheelie bins.'

'And did you?'

'I couldn't possibly say.' He smirked.

'Urgh! She was ancient.'

'Nah, she was like thirty-five, tops!'

Will took a drag and shook his head slowly. 'Come on, let's get going.'

The boys jostled for position in the car, snare drums, amps and guitars on their laps. Jake, riding shotgun, rolled down the window and flicked on the radio; it struggled for reception for a moment, before settling down on 'Karma Chameleon.'

They made their way slowly back to the estate, rows of terraced houses with shiny new satellite dishes flanking the village green. Pete dropped them off one by one – the car thankful for each shedding of weight.

Will headed up the gravelled driveway, kicking the loose stones with his toes, before turning his key in the door. It was a little after eleven and his mother, Helen, was passed out on the couch, having fallen asleep during a rerun of *Absolutely Fabulous*. He surveyed the coffee table with disdain – an empty bottle of wine and the sorry remains of a microwave curry. He scooped them up in his hands, took them through to the kitchen, threw them in the bin and headed upstairs. He made a token gesture of cleaning his teeth and got into bed, still fully clothed. The ceiling was spinning in a jerky waltz. He stared at it for a moment, trying to steady it, before shutting his eyes and drifting off to sleep.

CHAPTER 2

A single beam of sunlight filtered through the blinds of the common room. It was the last week of college and sparks of excitement for the summer ahead ricocheted around the room.

Will sat with the others in the corner, rucksacks at their feet. They had neither the inclination nor the reputation to move the first-years from the better tables. He wore a frayed navy jumper with sleeves so long they covered his bony hands – a style he hoped looked more Kurt Cobain than errant toddler. With a marker pen, he scribbled out the set list to go through at that afternoon's rehearsal.

No Love Lost
Reduced to Routine
Waiting for Nothing
Midnight Sun
Distant Days
Vital Signs

With a critical eye, he double-checked that he'd written the same order for everyone; he didn't want a repeat of the time Luke counted them in and they all started playing different songs.

'How much are we getting paid on Friday?' Luke asked, his dry blond hair looking like it might combust in the radiant sun.

'Depends on how many people come along.'

'So, fuck all?'

Will laughed, unsure whether a factual statement could actually be considered a joke.

'Nah, last day of term – every man and his dog will be out,' said Jake, running his fingers through his fringe.

Luke narrowed his gaze. 'Dog?'

'Tamagotchi, then.' He grinned.

A group of kids with too much gel in their hair cranked 'California Love' by 2Pac up on the stereo.

Jake glared at them. 'This music's shite. Look at them all nodding their heads. I bet none of them have even been to California.'

'And you have, I suppose?' asked Pete, his head shaved to a number three and features unapologetically angular.

'No, but I don't fucking sing about it, do I?'

'No – you sing what Will tells you to sing.'

Will forced a smile, inwardly pleased with the power bestowed upon him.

A group of popular girls chatted away giddily about who was wearing what to the party at the weekend – a party the boys evidently weren't invited to. Will tried to block them out, telling himself that he didn't want to go anyway.

As the bell sounded, Luke and Pete gathered up their things and started to trudge towards the exam hall.

'See you in the music room after!' Jake shouted.

'You knows it!' Pete hollered back.

*

The equipment in the practice room was distinctly Tesco voucher. The red Mapex drum kit seemed to be getting smaller with each practice and the stool squeaked every time Luke moved. An overworked rotary fan whirred away, spewing out welcome blasts of cool air. Luke tightened up the rattly snare while Will fiddled with the bass and treble knobs on the tiny Peavey amp, strumming an A minor between each minute adjustment.

'Yo, yo, yo! Testing, one-two, one-two!' barked Jake into the microphone in an accent that wasn't quite his own.

Every session started the same: everyone playing separate songs, in different keys, 'to get the tone they wanted', culminating in a horrible cacophony of noise, until somebody finally said, 'Right, shall we play a number, then?'

'I'm gonna miss this old place,' said Jake, tapping the low dusty ceiling with the palm of his hand.

'Yeah, it'll be good to start using proper equipment somewhere else, though,' said Will, plugging his mic into the mixer with a crackle of static.

Pete arrived late, clutching the local free paper under his arm, a gigantic smile invading his face. 'Did you guys see this? We got a review in *The Herald.*' He spread out the paper on the drum kit and hastily thumbed through it, past the classified ads for second-hand cars and unwanted furniture, towards the entertainment section.

Silent Emergency, SharpShooter and Crimson Oath – The Jolly Monkey

Taking to the stage second, SharpShooter played a punchy set full of heart. Rather than sucking on the fag end of Britpop, these boys have shunned their parents' Beatles records for a sound reminiscent of the Pixies and Radiohead, combined with the melodic ear of REM. Singer Jake Summers' voice soars over guitarist Will Green's impressive guitar work, while rhythm section Pete Easton and Luke Taylor pound away with youthful energy. File these guys under 'ones to watch'.

'Fucking 'ell – told you we played well,' Jake exclaimed, snatching the paper.

'Love that,' said Luke.

Will read it over again, wanting to savour every word but also anxious that they should get on with the rehearsal.

When they eventually got going, the grubby walls of the music room reverberated with their glorious racket. Riffs and beats collided violently in the air as they played extra loud and fast, as if to affirm their new-found 'ones to watch' status.

'We need to get this one down on tape,' panted Jake after 'No Love Lost'.

'I'm not sure we're ready,' Will cautioned.

'Oh, piss off. Course we are!'

Pete played a snippet of 'The Chain' on his bass, before muting the strings with his hand. 'We're getting there,' he said with a smile. Pete was, by his own admission, the least musical of the band. He'd originally joined as an excuse to hang out and smoke with his mates but had since grown into a competent, if unorthodox, bass player. Will had hamfistedly taught him to play, but the student soon outstripped his master. He was no longer just hammering away at root notes but now playing with real verve and grace.

After the session, they each grabbed a stodgy burger from the canteen and headed into town, chatting with their mouths full as they made their way up the hill. They passed teenage girls with pencil-thin eyebrows pushing prams, a grizzly busker butchering 'Knocking on Heaven's Door' and the fountain littered with kids in hoodies, before arriving at Tony's – the only decent record store in town.

The bell chimed as they pushed open the door. Tony, wispy-haired, stubbly and wearing a My Bloody Valentine T-shirt two sizes too small, welcomed them in.

'All right, Tone,' said Jake, entering first and striding towards the counter.

The others dispersed throughout the shop, each finding their own little niche. Will flicked through the new CD releases, reading their little handwritten descriptions, while Pete browsed the rock and pop vinyl – the artwork large and magical. Luke thumbed through the soul and funk section. His father had been the drummer in function bands around the town in the 80's and had taught him to play from an early age. Luke had chanced upon Will and Jake's advert on the college noticeboard and was happy to ride in the duo's slipstream.

Jake rummaged around in his rucksack and pulled out some tatty scraps of paper. 'We've got some flyers for our gig on Friday, if we can leave them here?'

Tony nodded. 'Sure. You boys ever going to buy anything, though?'

'One day, Tone, one day.'

Will continued to leaf through the CDs, but out of the corner of his eye he noticed a dark-haired girl at the listening station. She was facing away from him, her scarlet top baring pale shoulders and giant earmuff headphones engulfing her head. He watched her for a moment, drawn to the way she bobbed her head gently to the beat.

'Who's that?' he whispered to Tony.

Tony shrugged. 'Not sure. She comes in quite a bit, though.'

'What's she listening to?'

'The Seahorses, I think. Squire's guitar work is top-notch, as you'd expect, but most of the songs aren't up to much.'

The girl turned her head slightly, revealing dimpled cheeks and delicate purple eyeshadow. Will allowed himself to daydream for a moment about what he might say to her. How they might connect over their favourite bands and obscure B-sides. Who was he kidding? He wouldn't speak to her. He would only stare and wonder. Suddenly, Pete snapped him abruptly back to reality.

'Will, your sister's outside.'

'What?' Will rushed towards the doorway. 'Izzy, what are you doing here?'

'Mum forgot to pick me up from school again,' she whimpered.

Will swallowed hard. 'Why didn't you get the bus home?'

She looked up at him, all sunshine-blonde curls and snotty nose. 'I didn't have any money,' she sniffed. 'I guessed I might find you here.'

'Come here.' He took her hand, clammy and small, in his. 'Boys, I'd better go. I'll see you Friday.'

CHAPTER 3

Amy sat cross-legged on her bedroom floor, straightening her hair. The faint smell of burning infiltrated her nostrils as she repeatedly ran the hot irons over her long dark locks. Tattered posters, ticket stubs and Polaroids adorned the walls as the early-evening sun created little pools of light on the carpet. Charlotte flicked through Amy's modest CD collection, landing on Catatonia and impatiently forcing the disc into the player.

'You nearly done yet, Ames? It's a gig, not a fashion parade.'

'How long did you take to get ready before you came over?'

'Not the point.' Charlotte smiled. She pulled some cigarette papers out of her handbag and began to roll on her lap.

'You can't smoke in here – my dad will kill me.'

'Chill out, it's for the walk. You want one?'

Amy shook her head dismissively.

'We need to get a head start on this too,' said Charlotte, pulling out a small bottle of vodka and pouring it into her glass of Coke, before grabbing Amy's and doing the same. 'Who's on tonight anyway?' she asked.

Amy reached for the photocopied flyer on the floor and slid it across to Charlotte, who scanned the angular serif font.

'SharpShooter.'

'I've heard they're pretty good,' said Amy.

'Well, let's get a move on then, shall we?'

Charlotte paced around the room, all unkempt red curls and slender, striking features. She scanned Amy's bookcase and yanked a random paperback off the shelf. She flicked through it, awakening its musty smell. She read a sentence out loud in a mockingly posh voice before putting it back.

'Do you actually read for fun, Amy?'

'Why else would you read?'

Charlotte shrugged. 'Cos it's on the syllabus?'

'How do I look?' asked Amy, standing to reveal her indigo blue denim skirt and black Ramones T-shirt, tied up at her midriff.

Charlotte gave her an appraising up and down. 'Like a slut, but a studious one. That's the look you were going for, yeah?'

'Naturally,' replied Amy, smiling. She sprayed some perfume in the air, waited a moment and walked into its cloud, the cold, scented droplets cooling her cheek. 'How'd you think you did with the exam earlier?'

'Shit. You?'

'All right, I guess,' said Amy bashfully.

Charlotte raised her glass in the air and swirled around the fizzy black liquid. 'That's the great thing about alcohol –

it can be used for both celebrating and drowning sorrows. It's Waffley versatile.'

'Waffley?'

'It's from an advert. Never mind – I forgot you're not allowed to watch telly.'

'I am so!' said Amy indignantly.

Charlotte downed her drink and placed the glass down on the desk. 'Come on, let's get out of here.'

Amy glanced at herself in the mirror and pushed stop on the stereo. She reached for her leather jacket, zipping it up to avoid an unwelcome critique of her outfit from her father, and the pair headed downstairs.

*

Will stuck the old white bedsheet masquerading as a backdrop to the wall with masking tape. At the third attempt, it stayed put. He jumped down from the tiny raised-platform stage and surveyed his handiwork – straight enough, and the crudely stencilled SharpShooter logo just about legible.

The Griffin was the largest pub in town. A drinkers' pub during the week, it put on live music on Friday and Saturday nights. Popular with college kids for its lax attitude to drinking laws, it exuded the permanent smell of badly casked ales and overcooked Pukka pies.

Jake adjusted his mic to the right height and tapped it twice with his finger to check it was working, two thuds rebounding back at him. 'It's weird, isn't it, for the first time since we were five years old, we are actually free to do what we like,' he said to no one in particular.

Luke shrugged. 'I know I've flunked my exams, so not sure I'll be that free to do anything, to be honest.'

Will shot Pete a sideways glance. They both knew he was full of crap when it came to college work, or lack of it.

Jake baulked. 'Doesn't matter, mate, you don't need qualifications to hit things for a living.'

Luke flashed him a cautious smile and began to attach his cymbals, sliding them down over the shining metal stands and screwing them in place.

Moments later, the landlord – a portly man with a scruffy goatee – came over to give them two paper drink tokens each. 'You're the only band on tonight. Got an acoustic act opening, then you guys can play for as long as you like.'

Jake looked at Luke. 'No, that doesn't mean you can do a fucking drum solo.'

'You try and stop me.' He cackled.

An hour or so later, the pub began to fill up. Two beardy guys sat on stools, staring at their feet, singing maudlin songs about the moon and the stars. Excitable kids babbled away over the music – the boys all Fred Perry polos and Lynx Africa, the girls all pale bare flesh and crunchy moussed hair.

Will, Jake, Pete and Luke stood to the side, feeling the palpable air of anticipation. Will's stomach quivered as the duo announced it was their last song, and he began to uncase his guitar.

SharpShooter took to the sweltering stage to rapturous applause from the well-oiled crowd. Will hit the top string of his guitar with the thumb of his right hand and shielded the LCD of his tuner from the stage lights with his left. He could just about make out the needle flickering intermittently between E and F. *Why will it never go in tune for a gig?* He turned the machine head clockwise, slowly moving the dial slightly. Suddenly, the DJ dipped the music and the house lights came down.

'We're SharpShooter – and school's out for summer!' bellowed Jake into the microphone.

The crowd squealed, Will thrashed at the opening chord of 'No Love Lost' and they were off. What followed next was a blur of flashing lights and frenetic energy. The jittery kids elbowed their way to the front, slopping their drinks everywhere as they jumped in time to Luke's pulsing beat – a tangle of limbs moving as one.

Jake looked out at them all and turned to Will, beaming from ear to ear. Pete turned his back to the audience, locking eyes with Luke, his driving bassline rumbling beneath it all.

During 'Midnight Sun', the obligatory slowie, Will looked out at the audience, goofily waving their lighters in the air. Through the throng of people he noticed a girl with long dark hair, arms around her friend, swaying gently to the beat.

It's the girl from the record store.

He looked down at the fretboard and picked away at the chorus, before looking out at her again – her cherry-red lips and makeup model eyes – she was the most beautiful vision he'd ever seen.

As the song lilted to an end, the pair headed off to the bar. Will, momentarily distracted, focused and kicked into the opening riff of the next song, and the kids were bouncing again. Jake, dripping with sweat, let his voice soar as the song climaxed to a mess of crashing cymbals and wailing feedback. The clambering crowd cried for an encore. They'd exhausted their repertoire so played a loose cover of 'Teenage Kicks', pounding away at the signature riff as the kids went berserk.

It was one of those nights which made all the crap that came with being in a band – the lugging of gear, the petty arguing, the organising of kit shares – feel absolutely worth it. Luke, getting carried away, threw his sticks out into the audience, hitting a chubby underage girl in the face and offering a hand of apology as he stepped off the stage.

Will clattered his gear away and leapt off the stage into the grabby crowd – he ignored their hands. He *had* to find the girl he'd seen.

As the DJ kicked into 'Laid', the kids splintered off into groups to dance. The guys stood at the bar, and Will's eyes searched around for her. Conversations between the others swirled around in the air, Will unable to tether himself to them.

He turned his head ninety degrees to the left, and there she was, stood three deep at the bar. She looked in his direction and smiled. Will was fairly certain it wasn't for him but smiled back anyway – a non-committal half-smile that could be passed off as a facial tic if need be.

'You guys were good!' she shouted over the noise.

'Thanks!' Will stuttered, moving closer. 'We aren't that good,' he added with faux nonchalance.

'Well, I thought you were.'

'That's very kind of you.' He shook his head – *too formal*.

'I liked the fast one. *I want nothing, I want nothing*,' she sang.

'It's waiting for nothing,' Will corrected her, with a pedantry he instantly hated himself for.

'You reminded me a bit of The Cure. I mean, a shit version of The Cure, obviously.' She laughed.

Will fiddled with the neck of his T-shirt, catching an unpleasant whiff of himself. 'The Cure. I'll take that.' He smiled, committing fully this time.

'What's your name?'

He moved his mouth closer to her ear, accidentally brushing her hair with his cheek. 'Will.'

'I'm Amy.'

Will looked at her. A fraction too long. 'Who you here with?'

'My friend Charlotte.' She pointed towards the back of the room. 'She's the one over there with her tongue down the throat of your singer.'

'Oh, shit,' muttered Will.

Amy ran her fingers through the back of her hair. 'Is he trouble?'

'No comment.'

Amy grinned. 'I reckon she can handle him.'

Both of them searched for something to say, the thumping beat of the music filling the silence between them.

'You can get me a drink if you like?'

Will smiled at her forwardness. 'Sure.'

He ordered her a Southern Comfort and lemonade, and a double Jack Daniels and Coke for himself. Having used his tokens long ago, he handed over most of his split of their fee.

'Cheers,' said Amy, clinking their glasses together.

Will was aware by now that Luke and Pete were watching him, nudging each other and laughing. His cheeks burnt a fierce red and trying to stop it only made it worse.

20

'I better be getting back to the guys,' he said, gesturing towards them.

'Oh, really. Well, maybe come find me later, yeah?'

Will nodded, attempting to play it cool and ignoring the ripple of excitement that passed through him. 'Will do.'

He headed back to the others, trying to look unfazed, as if this kind of thing happened to him all the time but failing spectacularly.

Girls had never really noticed him before, particularly not with the company he kept. He'd struggled with acne since his early teens, but his skin was finally beginning to clear up and he'd grown out his unflattering French crop into a mop of tousled brown curls.

Jake used to tease him about whether he'd ever kissed a girl, or 'titted one up', to the point that it became easier to invent holiday romances or fictional rendezvous with girls who 'go to a different school' than tell him the truth that, besides a couple of snogs at youth club, his slate was clean. He sometimes wondered whether being 'alternative' was really just the *alternative* to being popular.

As the DJ soldiered on with Britpop crowd-pleasers, Will chanced a few glances to his left to check that Amy was still there. She knew he would be doing so but pretended to be too deep into the music to notice. It was all Will could think about – the tiny promise of something good.

The music washed over him as he danced uneasily from foot to foot. He looked over at Jake, still pashing Charlotte – effortlessly cool in a sketchy, punk-rock way – against the back wall and tried to curb his rising jealousy.

Last orders were called and the kids were ushered out, waddling as their shoes stuck to the cider-stained floor. It was dark outside, but the air was warm, the kind of balmy evening that reminded Will of Spanish holidays with his mum and dad as a child.

He could see Amy and Charlotte up ahead, making a beeline for a taxi that was pulling up. He felt his hazy vision narrow and became acutely aware that any chance he had was, at that very moment, slipping away.

'Hey,' he said croakily.

'Oh, it's you,' said Amy, a reassuring flicker of a smile on her face.

'Where are you two heading now? We're having an after-party.'

The rest of the band looked at Will, wondering quite how he planned to pull an after-party out of his arse.

'Home. We've got this taxi booked. But here, take this.' Amy unclenched her fist and passed him a crumpled piece of tissue, her phone number scrawled on it in black eyebrow pencil.

Will's eyes scanned the digits. 'Thanks. I'll call you.'

'That's the idea,' Amy teased; her words trailed off as they clambered into the back of the taxi. Will waved them off. Jake, Luke and Pete did the same behind his back, mockingly blowing kisses.

'Come on then, lover boy, time to go,' said Jake.

On the car ride home, the euphoria of the evening gave way to a tired silence. Will pulled the tissue out from his pocket and smoothed it out in his hand. He looked at it in the amber glow of passing streetlights and smiled to himself.

Amy 01632 523471 x

CHAPTER 4

Amy sat on the bed, her back against the headboard, cradling a mug of tea in her hands. It was an overcast Sunday evening and the muggy air crept in through the partially open window. Billy Corgan snarled away on the stereo. She flicked through the latest *Melody Maker*, the thick black ink smudging on her thumbs.

'Amy! Phone for you,' her mum called from downstairs.

'Who is it?'

'Someone called Will.'

Amy scampered downstairs. Glowing red, she snatched the phone, covered the earpiece with the palm of her left hand and shooed her curious mother off into the kitchen. It had taken Will nearly forty-eight hours to muster the courage to call, and he was mortified when her mum had answered instead.

'Hi, it's… er… Will.'

'Well, hi there, *er, Will.*' Amy giggled. 'I thought you might never call.'

'Course I would,' he stammered. 'Do you go to sixth form? Not seen you around.'

'No. Girls' grammar. The college part. Don't worry, I'm not like fifteen or something. No jailbait here, sir.'

Will laughed uneasily and searched for what to say next.

'I'll make this simple for you, shall I?' said Amy, nipping the silence in the bud. 'Would you like to take me out sometime?'

'Yes, I'd like that,' Will replied eagerly. 'How about Wednesday evening?'

'Pick me up from outside the gates?'

'Sure, it'll have to be a backy on my bike, though.' Will winced.

'Walking's fine.' Amy laughed.

'Cool. See you Wednesday.'

*

Will placed the cordless back on the receiver. He prayed that Izzy hadn't been listening on the other line. He slumped back on the bed, a tiny tingle of excitement passing through him – *it was a date*.

Moments later, his mum shouted up the stairs that Jake was at the door. Will hollered down for her to let him up.

Jake bowled into the room, greasy dark hair shooting out from under a yellow beanie. 'Here, have this,' he said, wrenching the cap off a bottle of beer with his teeth and handing it to him. 'How's it going with that girl from Friday night?'

'Amy? I just called her…'

24

'And?'

'We are going out Wednesday night.'

'Nice, where you taking her?'

'I'm not sure yet.'

'You should take her swimming – see what she looks like with no makeup on early doors. You don't want that shit to be a surprise.'

Will scowled. He fiddled with the cord of his hoodie, enjoying the sensation of the knotted fabric running through his fingers. 'You gonna call her friend?'

'Nah. Ain't got time for girls right now.'

'Yeah, practically a monk.' Will smirked.

'Oh, by the way, my old man says we can practise in the garage now we can't use the music room. He said he'd get us a shitty PA and I could work it off on the site.'

Will took another sip of beer and placed it down gently on the bedside table. 'That's awesome. Be good to have our own space, work on some new stuff.'

Jake looked at him intently – he had a magnetism Will could neither define nor deny. 'This is our moment, Will. We can blow most of the other bands in this town out of the water. You know that.' He took another glug of beer and clinked the bottle against Will's.

'The future is ours, mate.'

*

Will looked himself up and down in the bathroom mirror and sprayed some cheap 'sporty' deodorant under his arms. He patted down his wet hair and straightened the collar of his green and black plaid shirt. He checked his watch, a digital Casio he could no longer remember if he was wearing ironically or not. He'd better get going. He had decided to take Amy for pizza, because everybody likes pizza, right?

He loaded a battered tape of *Crooked Rain* into his Walkman and bumped his way through rush hour towards the girls' grammar. Sunlight glistened on the bonnets of stationary cars eager to get home. A little over an hour out of London, Malford was a town struggling for identity. The leafy suburbs papered over the cracks of mass unemployment and boarded-up shops that punctuated the high street. Industrial units now lay empty and graffiti-ridden, as many of the town's traditional exports – cars, canned foods and electronics – were now being produced more cheaply abroad.

The gates of the grammar school were gaudy and imposing. He tried to guess what the Latin motto 'Mentem Frontem Que' meant. *Probably something to do with courage*, he thought.

Amy was waiting outside for him, a black denim jacket over a white T-shirt, chewing on gum and stealthily checking herself out in a pocket mirror. She hastily threw it in her handbag as she noticed Will approaching.

'Ah, we meet again.' She beamed.

'We do,' replied Will, smiling the biggest smile he would allow himself.

'Where are you taking me, then? There better be food involved.'

'Oh, there is, don't you worry,' he replied, relaxing a little and gesturing with an open hand for her to follow him.

*

26

Paolo's was quiet. Too quiet. The pungent smell of garlic circulated in the air-conditioning and the strip lighting flickered erratically. Will slid his clammy fingers across the laminated menu.

'Pictures of the food – the hallmark of quality.'

'I'm a lucky girl.' Amy smiled.

With impeccable timing, the waiter arrived to take their order. Will figured a beer would really take the edge off things right now so chanced ordering a pint, and a glass of white wine for Amy, planning to just wing it if the waiter asked for ID. They chose a 'Mega Meat' pizza to share, and he hoped the money his mum had given him would cover it all. God knows it was embarrassing enough asking for it.

'So, what bands do you like?' asked Will, tapping anxiously on the table with a breadstick.

'Um, Suede, Smashing Pumpkins, Nirvana, Ash – loads, really. What's your band called again?'

'SharpShooter,' Will replied, stopping himself from reciting Jake's spiel about the name. 'Do you play yourself?'

'Do I play with myself? *How dare you*? That's a little forward for a first date, don't you think?'

'I-I didn't say that...'

'I'm teasing. No, I don't play any instruments, if that's what you asked. I read a lot, I write a bit and I run.'

'Run? Urgh. I hate running.'

Amy took a sip of the table water. 'You should try it. Put some music on and just run. It's like for that moment nothing else matters, you know?'

'I have the lung capacity of a seven-year-old – that would matter, surely?'

'Is that why you can't sing?' Amy replied, sticking out her tongue.

Will clutched his hand to his chest, feigning hurt.

'I saw you chipping in on the second mic. I thought it was cute. Did you see me?'

'You can't see much because of the lights,' he fibbed.

Amy fiddled with her serviette, folding it and unfolding again. 'What's the plan for the band, then?'

'I dunno. We're recording a demo soon hopefully. Gonna send it to places in London, see what happens.'

Amy nodded with genuine warmth in her eyes. 'But what do you want out of it?'

Will had never been asked this before and it took him aback. 'I don't know. I just want to create something, something good. Something that moves people, you know?'

Amy looked up from her plate and stared him straight in the eye. 'Will.'

'What?'

'Promise me you'll *never* write a song about me.'

'I can't promise that, I'm afraid,' he said with a smile.

The food arrived and they stopped chatting momentarily as the waiter put down the plates, as if what they were saying would be of any interest to him.

'Where do you live?' asked Amy.

'On the Grantham estate.'

Will was certain that she'd know of its reputation, but Amy remained poker-faced.

'It's just me, my mum and sister,' he continued.

'Do you still see your dad?'

Will swallowed, slowly. 'No. He died a couple of years ago.'

'Oh, I'm sorry to hear that,' said Amy, and she really seemed to mean it, unlike a lot of people he told about his father.

Will picked at an imaginary bit of lint on his sweater. 'It's OK. It's been tough on my mum, but she's getting better... we both are.'

Amy reached over and put her hand on his. 'Sorry if this is an awful question, but how did he die?'

'Heart attack. On the factory floor at work. Only forty-six.' His voice caught in the air. He looked up at Amy, who held his gaze. 'We didn't really have a chance to get used to the idea. Just one day he was here, and the next he wasn't.' Will wafted his hands in front of his eyes. 'Anyway, heavy stuff for a first date. Who was your friend at the gig?'

'Charlotte. She's great.' Amy's face lit up as she spoke.

Will nodded and took a slice of pizza, the toppings slid off as he did, so he scooped them up with his fingers, before giving Amy a messy grin.

'Tell your singer to call her. He doesn't know what he's missing out on.'

Will shrugged. 'I'll try, but I can't promise anything. Jake kinda does what he likes.'

*

After dinner, Will walked Amy home. He walked on the outside of her. He'd been told it was considered chivalrous but wasn't sure why. She lived on the outskirts of town, on 'The Posh', as the band called it.

Approaching the gates, Will winced remembering the time that he and Jake had drunkenly pissed on them in a

29

half-arsed act of rebellion. As they walked a little further, he dangled out his hand in the hope she might hold it, and she did. His knuckles clenched to white, her hand warm inside his.

'This is me,' said Amy, pointing to a large beige house with thick ivy trailing down the front. 'Thank you for a great evening.'

Amy moved her face closer to his; Will closed his eyes, his chances of a kiss hanging by a thread.

Suddenly, there was an abrasive double tap on the window, followed by the stirring of the curtains.

'Shit. It's my dad. It's late – I'd better go.' She pecked him on the cheek and disappeared towards the house.

Will watched her walk up the drive for as long as he could.

She turned back, briefly. 'Call me.'

CHAPTER 5

Will leant sullenly against the outside wall of RollerZone, hands in his jeans pockets, pulling at a loose thread. A slight chill filled the air and he regretted not bringing a jacket. He checked his watch. Amy was twenty-two minutes late; he began to fret about whether she was still coming. He'd had a swig of vodka from the drinks cabinet at home for some Dutch courage and could still feel the warm sting in his throat.

A string of young couples went in; it was clear that they'd be the oldest people there by some years. He avoided eye contact with them; he couldn't bear the sympathy glances from those who thought he'd been stood up.

A jumble of litter swirled around on the dirty breeze. A swarm of Year Nines in shiny two-piece tracksuits congregated on the corner, throwing greasy chips at each other and cackling with laughter. Will's mind flitted back to the time at school when Jake had convinced him to bunk off to the chip shop for lunch. He'd enjoyed the thrill, until they got caught by a teacher on patrol and put in after-school detention. Looking back, he didn't really see the point as they served chips in the canteen anyway.

Moments later, Amy arrived in a flurry of apology. Will brushed it off, silently relieved that he hadn't been left hanging. He hugged her clumsily and kissed her gently on the cheek. He wasn't sure if he was meant to kiss both, like they did in French films, but she didn't offer up the second one.

'How are your skating skills, Will?'

'Used to come here when I was younger, but not for years now. It's crappy, I know, but should be fun.'

He thought skating was a solid second date, one that gave the impression he was adventurous and carefree – a charade he planned to keep up for as long as possible.

'Well, don't be grabbing onto me, unless you want us both to stack it.' She smiled. The pair filtered their way into the queue. 'I'll get this,' said Amy, handing over a crisp £20.

'What Is Love' blared out of the speaker system as they tentatively rolled their way out onto the polished wooden floor, a prism of lights swirling merrily around. Boys in thick white Fila jumpers, Adidas poppers and gelled curtains whizzed around the circuit, cockily skating backwards and busting 360s as the girls watched on.

The whole thing felt like a primitive mating ritual – one Will wanted no part of. The boys sniggered as he held on to the railings and tried to keep up with Amy, who was growing in confidence. His face burning up, he let go of the side and pushed himself off.

'Look at you go, Christopher Dean!' Amy laughed.

'He was an ice skater!' shouted Will over the music.

'Name one famous roller skater, then?'

'Touché.'

Slowly but steadily, Will began to find his stride. He reached out his clammy hand and Amy took hold of it, her head level with the top of his shoulders. He gripped it tightly as she picked up speed and pulled him along, gliding majestically across the shiny surface.

After a few laps, they stopped for a breather, sitting down on the benches by the side of the circuit. Amy took a swig of Fanta Orange and stifled a burp with her hand. A spotty boy in a red hoodie approached them nervously.

'You in SharpShooter?'

Will looked at him, startled. 'Yeah.'

'I saw you play a few weeks ago. You guys rock!'

'Cheers,' replied Will, trying to look nonplussed as the boy scurried back to his friends.

Amy looked at him with an arched eyebrow. 'Will, if I find out he was a plant, then I'm never speaking to you again.'

Will raised his palms up defensively. 'Never seen him before in my life, honest.' He laughed.

Amy leant in towards him, her face so close to his that he could feel her warm breath. 'Sorry about my dad the other night. He's always had *the* worst timing.'

'It's OK.'

'You can kiss me later if you like.' She grinned mischievously.

'What is this? Year Six?' joked Will, although in truth he actually quite liked her spelling things out for him.

'Judging by the standard of your skating, yeah.'

'Fair one.' He looked at her – those startling blue eyes and flawless rose skin – and leant forward to kiss her. As

33

he did so, the staccato piano of 'Alright' crashed in over the speakers.

'I love this song! Come on!' shrilled Amy, springing back to her feet and out onto the floor.

Will gave a knowing glance to a camera that wasn't there, before gingerly getting up and skating after her.

The DJ transitioned into 'Girls and Boys', the bouncy bassline making Will feel a little bolder as he glided around the corners. He skated off sharply, confident that Amy would follow.

'Slow down!' Amy called after him.

Will spun around to face her.

Smack!

He smashed straight into a weaselly-looking kid skating full speed behind him. There was a sickening crunch of nose on forehead as they collided and Will thudded to the ground. He lay motionless on his back, staring up at the fluorescent lights for a moment, the warm air of skaters whooshing by, before passing out.

He awoke groggily a few minutes later. A small room with white walls faded into focus. The smell of detergent and TCP filled his nostrils. He tried to piece together where he was, and who he was; his head felt like it was inside a tumble dryer, that much he knew. He seemed to be sitting upright but couldn't be sure.

'Aw, there he is,' said Amy, her features slowly emerging through the haze.

Will looked down at his top and saw that it was covered in crimson. 'What happened?'

'You got a bit overzealous on your skates, started doing flips, landed on your head.'

'What?'

'Sorry, no, that's not true. You collided with some kid going the other way.'

'Is he OK?'

'He's fine. Here, hold this to your nose and tip your head back,' she said, handing him a fresh tissue.

'Is it broken?'

'I doubt it. You'll have a nice bruise tomorrow, though, I reckon.'

Will pushed the physical pain to one side for a moment and focused on his pride – equally as bruised.

'I'm sorry. You must think I'm an idiot,' he said.

'You're kidding. I wouldn't miss this for the world.' She laughed, gently stroking his hair.

'Thanks.' He tried to smile, but the shooting pain through his nose put paid to the idea.

'How's he doing?' asked a balding man in a green St John Ambulance uniform.

'He'll live,' said Amy.

'Your girlfriend's done a great job of looking after you,' said the man.

Will cringed at the word 'girlfriend'. He liked the sound of it but felt awkward on Amy's behalf. She didn't recoil in horror or correct him though, which he hoped must count for something.

'Have some water,' said the man, handing him a small plastic cup, cool to the touch. 'I've got to go and deal with a boy who's banged his knee, but are you OK getting home?'

They both nodded. Amy looked at Will, a tissue in his nose, blood on his shirt. Aware of how ridiculous he must look, he avoided her eye.

'It's a story, I guess,' he said with a half-smile.

Amy adjusted her bobby pin and wiped her dirty hands on a paper towel. 'Will – look at me.'

Will turned his head slowly to face her and held her gaze for as long as he dared. She leant over and kissed him. Her lips were warm and soft as they met his. A tingle of elation passed through him as he put his hand on the small of her back and kissed her, his tongue lingering. He moved his head back away from hers, separating their lips.

'That was nice.'

'*Nice* – is that all I get? I thought you were a wordsmith, Will?'

'I've just had a blow to the head – cut me some slack.'

Amy offered her hand and levered him up from the chair. 'Come on then, let's get you home.'

*

Will turned his key in the lock, wiped each foot twice on the doormat and stepped inside. His sister came bolting towards him.

'Izzy. It's gone ten. What you doing up?'

'Mum's in bed. I've not had dinner yet.'

Will looked at her. Her eyes were red and puffy. He could tell that she'd been crying.

'I tried to make some jam on toast, but I burnt it.'

Will patted her gently on the head. 'I'll make you something, then straight to bed, OK?'

'What happened to your face?' she asked.

'Long story.'

Will scanned the fridge – nothing. He grabbed a tin of

baked beans from the cupboard and cackhandedly opened it with the metal tin opener. He wished his dad was still here, then he wouldn't have to deal with this crap. He allowed himself to think about him for a moment. His beardy, spectacled face and long hairy arms – he'd have known what to say to get Mum out of bed.

He fixed Izzy a child-sized portion of beans on toast and finished off the rest of the tin himself. She wolfed it down with a Ribena chaser and hugged him tightly as he scraped the remains into the bin. He planted a solitary kiss on her cheek; something he'd never done before.

'Off to bed, you.'

CHAPTER 6

'We are SharpShooter. This one's called "Reduced to Routine", said Jake, calmly into the dented SM-58, before turning to Luke and nodding. Luke began to pound away on the toms, throwing in a crash at the beginning of each loop, feeling the shockwaves of the taut skins radiate through his wrists. Pete slid his index finger down the second string of his bass and joined in the groove with panache. Will stomped on his chunky yellow distortion box and threw his fingers into the circular pattern of the opening riff. The pokey venue filled with punters as they fired through the set. Those stood arms folded at the back were there to see local stalwarts Sawdust, who were on after, but there was a swelling number of kids at the front for them, pogoing and mouthing the words back at them.

'*These streets aren't paved with gold, they're stained with blood. Everything we had got lost in the flood,*' soared Jake over the howling noise. Will lifted his head from the fretboard and locked eyes with Amy in the crowd, feeling a flutter at the base of his chest. She was stood shoulder to shoulder with Charlotte, two rows back, nodding her head – tiny, almost indecipherable, movements that meant everything to him. Seeing her there made him giddy with joy, but a sense of trepidation also came with it, his hands trembled and moved as if independent from his body as he tried to concentrate on the changes. Jake lifted one foot up on to the monitor, the designer rip in the knee of his jeans opening up a little more. He swept his salty fringe out of his eyes and bashed the tambourine against his hip on the off-beat to hysterical whoops from a gaggle of girls with studded belts, leopard print and badly dyed hair. Goaded by his rowdy mates, a lardy boy stage-bombed into the crowd as the final number descended into a swirl of feedback and flying pints.

'That was awesome!' said Amy as Will clambered off the stage and gave her a sweaty embrace.

'It felt good,' he replied, allowing himself a rare moment of pride. Will turned to the rest of the band. 'Guys, you remember Amy, don't you?'

'Hi,' they collectively mumbled.

'Charmed to make your acquaintance,' purred Jake, taking Amy's hand with a flourish and kissing it.

Will ignored the pang of resentment. Jake flopped down on the stage and stared up at Amy through his fringe. 'I hear you're quite the skater.'

'Ha, I wouldn't say that.' She smiled.

'Who wants a drink?' said Will, dragging Amy off to the bar before the conversation could go any further.

Jake turned to face Charlotte, stood there with her hands on her hips, olive-green eyeshadow and large silver hoop earrings shimmering in the stage lights.

'You didn't call.'

'Sorry, been super busy with the band and stuff.'

Charlotte ran her tongue over her teeth coquettishly. 'I don't believe you.'

Luke and Pete started to pack the gear away, pretending they weren't listening in. Jake stuffed his hands in his pockets and tapped the toes of his boots together.

'Look, I'm not looking for anything serious right now, but if you wanna hang out—'

'But you kissed me, that makes us an item, right?'

Jake squinted at Charlotte's face as she eventually grinned. 'Hanging out's cool.'

Sawdust took to the stage, the singer patrolling it assuredly in a tatty green anorak and oversized shades. Will stood languidly at the bar with Amy. He took the plunge and put his arm around her, and she didn't shake it off. He ordered a Southern Comfort and lemonade for Amy, a Malibu and Coke for Charlotte, and a pint for himself.

'Have you got any ID?' asked the barman with a greasy ponytail and black T-shirt with illegible yellow lettering on it.

'No, but I was in the band that was just on,' replied Will.

'Doesn't matter, you've got to be eighteen to drink here.'

'So, you're happy for me to entertain others who are drinking, but not drink myself?' He felt like a dick even as he was saying it.

'Sixteen to play, eighteen to drink.'

'Well, I guess I'll have two Cokes and a lemonade then.'

'It's Pepsi.'

Will just glared at him. The barman picked up the little drinks gun and started to fizz it into the glasses, handing them over. They were not long out of the dishwasher and tepid in the palm of his hand.

'Screw this place,' said Amy as they walked back to join the boys. 'My friend Sarah's having a house party near mine if you fancy it? Her parents are in the South of France. Should be still going.'

'Yeah, let's get out of here.'

'Pete will drive us. We can swing by Safeway, get some booze,' said Jake.

'Will I?' Pete smirked.

'Pete, we both know you're going to.'

He did a quick head count. 'We won't all fit in the car.'

'That's what laps are for, Petey-Boy.'

He conceded a smile. 'Come on then.'

They loaded up the car with people and gear – more weight than it had seen before. Charlotte squeezed her petite frame in between Will and Jake in the back, and Amy climbed on Will's lap, kissing him on the lips as she sat herself down.

'Try not to get a stiffy,' whispered Jake, a little too accurately.

As the car pulled up to the party, legs were desperate to be stretched and drinks desperate to be drunk. The house was large and Georgian, with immaculate hedges and carefully tended flowerbeds. A solitary pool of sick lay in front of a garden gnome, as if he was fishing from a river of vomit. The woollen bass of the music inside thumped through the walls as they sauntered up the drive. The door was ajar, so they let themselves in.

'Amy, you made it!' gushed Sarah. The house reeked of weed and Snoop Dogg jabbered away on the stereo.

'Come on in, there's people I want you to meet,' said Sarah, taking them through to the living room. The gang grabbed a bottle of Hooch each from the carrier bag and perched on the edge of the sofa. Will surveyed the room. A boy in a blue blazer and unnecessary fedora was doing tedious magic tricks for two girls sitting cross-legged on the floor and a spotty lad in a Global Technacolour T-shirt moved to the music with all the grace of a harpooned whale.

'What is this crap?' said Jake, pointing to the stereo.

'Chill out, mate. They aren't going to be playing The Velvet Underground at a party, are they?' said Pete.

Amy, not feeling the vibe, wedged herself in next to Will. She put her lips to his ear and whispered, 'Let's go upstairs.'

'Why, what's upstairs?'

'Oh, Will, you're so naïve,' she said, kissing his neck.

Will's stomach lurched. He wasn't ready for this; he was too sober, too uptight, too fond. Amy pulled him up from the couch and led him by the hand out of the room. The boys gave each other knowing nudges, screeching to a halt when Charlotte clocked them.

The party, which had started out as a drinks-on-coasters affair, had since become a free-for-all. A boy was being 'antiqued' in the kitchen to howls of laughter, a smashed vase sat on the sideboard next to the telephone and muddy footprints blighted the stairs. The pair glided over them and rushed to the top of the house. Amy swung open the door to the first room on the left. A couple had got there before them, snogging heavily on the bed. She tried the bathroom opposite; Will was relieved when the locked door didn't budge.

'In here,' said Amy, flinging open the door next to it.

'Is this her parents' room?' said Will, agitated. 'I'm not sure about this.'

Amy pulled him in and kissed him in no uncertain terms. Her lips were sugary and damp as they grazed his.

Downstairs, a bottle of cheap tequila had been cracked open. Blazer Boy gave each person a jagged piece of lime and placed a shaker of salt on the table.

'Tequila!' he announced, making ceremonial trumpet noises with his lips.

A row of shots was lined up, the tiny glasses full to the brim with gold liquid.

'Do you know how to do them?' Blazer Boy asked.

Jake gave him a wry smile.

'Salt, tequila and then lime,' he continued anyway, looking Jake up and down with very little stealth.

Jake licked the side of his hand, poured a patch of salt onto it and readied the lime. 'Three, two, one – down it!'

Luke necked it whole, his face contorting until it had no discernible features. Jake snorted the salt, downed the tequila, then stuffed the whole lime wedge in his mouth and chewed. Blazer Boy stared at him with his mouth agape.

'Yuck!' a girl with peroxide-blonde hair screamed, spitting a huge mouthful of salt out onto the carpet.

'It's salt first!' howled Blazer Boy, bent over double with laughter. 'You don't usually spit out a salty mouthful until much later in the evening, Emma.'

'Fuck off, Greg!' she shrieked, running off to the downstairs toilet.

Upstairs, Will and Amy lay on the bed kissing feverishly.

She moved her hand slowly down his chest and began to fumble with his belt.

Will sat up suddenly. 'I can't, sorry, not here. It's just… it's just this room.'

'What about it?'

'It smells of old people.' He slid his belt back into its loop and flounced back down on the bed. 'I really like you, Amy, and I don't want our first time to be here… plus, anyone could walk in.'

Amy nodded solemnly. Will lay there, unsure if she was angry or not, but probed no further.

Back downstairs, Jake was swigging on his fifth Hooch, dancing loosely by the stereo. He looked at Pete and Luke sat on the couch. 'Come on, dance, you boring fuckers!'

Blazer Boy turned to his friend, buttoned-up shirt and painstakingly coiffured bouffant. 'Somebody's had too many E-numbers.'

'What was that?'

'Nothing.'

'Didn't sound like nothing.'

'Leave it, Jake,' Pete intervened.

'Nah, I'm sick of these guys. They've been looking down on us since we arrived.'

'Ha, if that's what you think…' Bouffant chipped in.

'We went to sixth form, you know,' said Jake.

'Well done, you,' deadpanned Blazer Boy. 'And what did you read?'

'What did I read? The *NME* and *Kerrang!* mainly,' sneered Jake.

'Very droll. I mean what did you study?'

'Well, fucking say that then, this isn't *University Challenge*.'

'Yeah, well, I don't think there's any chance of you appearing on that, don't worry.'

Jake felt his hackles begin to rise. 'And why would that be?'

'It's just that they only tend to have the top universities on it. Not polytechnics and such like.'

'Fuck you,' Jake snarled. They were up in each other's faces now.

'Fuck me? Why are you guys even here?'

'We know Amy and Charlotte.'

'Oh yeah, most guys do, if you know what I mean,' said Blazer Boy, turning to a sniggering Bouffant for approval.

'Don't say shit like that about them.'

Blazer Boy scoffed as Jake rushed forward, slamming him hard into the television, toppling it. A flurry of fists ensued, both boys scuffling around on the floor in a red mist.

'Fight! Fight!' shouted an impossibly tanned boy in a white baseball cap. People rushed in from the garden through the patio doors. Luke and Pete tried to drag Jake off, Bouffant clawing at their backs.

Will and Amy, hearing the commotion, dashed downstairs to see Jake, T-shirt ripped, being restrained by Luke. 'I'll fucking kill him!' he yelled, trying to force himself free. Blazer Boy's nose was dripping big splodges of claret on the plush cream carpet.

'What the hell's going on?' shouted Sarah.

'Ask him,' Blazer Boy whimpered, pointing at Jake.

'Amy,' said Sarah flatly, 'I think you guys better go.'

The gang quickly gathered up their stuff and headed for the door.

'For Christ's sake, Jake,' Will mumbled. 'What was that all about?'

'Nothing.'

'Nothing? So, you just punched him for no reason, did you? Great plan. Really great first impression.'

'The guy was a prick. Kept mouthing off.'

'About what?' Will seethed.

'Look, just leave it. You don't want to know,' said Jake, turning away from him. They piled into the Corsa and sat in stony silence. Pete turned the radio on to try and ease the mood; the Spice Girls blasted out.

'What the hell is a "zigazig ah" anyway?' asked Luke.

Will sighed. 'Not now, Luke. Not now.'

CHAPTER 7

Will shovelled some Pick 'n' Mix into a paper bag: fried eggs, flying saucers, strawberry laces and cola bottles. He weighed the bag in his left hand: 75p per 100g – he had no frame of reference for how much that was.

Amy threw in some jellybeans. 'I spoke to Sarah and she's finally calmed down about the party. Her parents were pretty pissed off about the damage, though.'

'Jake can be such an idiot sometimes.'

'Did he tell you what it was all about?'

Will twizzled the paper bag around to close it. 'No, he wouldn't say. He just said that I would have done the same had I been there. But I doubt it.'

Amy took a chilled bottle of Dr Pepper from the refrigerator and said nothing. They pooled their shrapnel and paid the cashier.

In the auditorium, under the light of the projector, Amy's teeth glowed vivid purple as Will counted freckles he'd never seen before on her face. She slid her hand into his bag of sweets and pulled out a sour cherry. The 20th Century Fox fanfare crashed in and Will put his hand on hers. Neither of them cared for *Men in Black* much. Will Smith and Tommy Lee Jones ran about in shades, trying their best, but the pair were too wrapped up in their own cynicism to be invested.

After the cinema, they walked arm in arm along the river towards the town centre. They passed the market traders packing down their stalls for the day and the early-evening drinkers in pubs that passed themselves off as wine lodges, and for that moment Will felt truly happy.

'Ah, shit, is that the time? I'm going to be late for practice,' he said, catching sight of the gaudy clock face above the town hall.

'I thought we were having dinner?'

'No time, sorry.'

Amy let go of his hand and it flopped limply down by his side.

'You're not annoyed, are you? asked Will.

'It's OK. I said I'd meet Charlotte for a drink later anyway,' said Amy flatly.

Will kissed her sharply on the cheek and legged it for the bus.

*

'Get here when you can,' said Jake, predictably, as Will slid open the shutters to the garage.

Will rolled his eyes to the others and grabbed his guitar. 'It's only ten past, chill out.'

Pete flicked his bass between clean and overdrive, trying to get the balance right, while Luke thumped out a random beat, forcing them all to shout over it. Will glanced around the garage: foam insulation on the walls, their own PA on stilts, a small white mini-fridge in the corner and their bedsheet banner pinned to the back wall.

'I like what you've done with the place.' He smiled.

'Yeah, my old man cleared all the crap out and put in a bit of soundproofing to keep the neighbours happy. He's filled the fridge with beers and snacks too.'

'Nice.' Will beamed.

Jake stubbed out his cigarette in an ashtray on top of the bass amp.

'I spoke to Tony. He poked his head into the gig the other night. He liked what he heard, said he'd put some money up for us to do a single, sell it at the shop – split everything fifty-fifty.'

'That's awesome!' gushed Pete.

The butterflies swirling in Will's stomach were welcome ones as he pulled some crumpled pages out of his guitar case. 'I've got a new thing I've been working on. It's called "The Outsiders". Just an idea at the mo, but I've got these chords for it.'

He strummed a D minor, letting it shimmer, followed by A minor, F and G. Pete joined in the second time around and Luke tentatively thumped the kick drum with his Adidas Sambas. Jake snatched the paper off the top of Will's amp and began to sing. '*You and me, we're The Outsiders, destined to dissolve, this feeling behind us.*'

Will joined in on the last line, elongating the word 'us', stomping on his fuzz pedal as Luke telepathically smashed the ride cymbals and threw himself headlong into a driving beat. Jake, feeling the groove, moved jerkily around the room, taking a stab at the second verse.

'Now it builds up to a big end refrain,' Will hollered over the swirling wall of noise.

'*And I'm close to heaven, when you call my name, and I'm close to heaven, do you feel the same?*' he wailed, his fragile voice not doing justice to the melody.

Jake wrapped the microphone cable around his wrists, took a deep breath and joined in an octave higher, elevating everything. Luke and Pete smiled at each other; they knew they were on the cusp of something special. Pete deviated away from the chords, adding some adventurous bass rolls, as Luke crashed away in a manner that even Animal from the Muppets might have considered over the top.

'Fuck, that was good!' panted Jake.

'That's the single!' said Pete.

'We can do it at SoundScene. The producer's meant to be good. He did Lightspeed's demo and it's the nuts,' said Luke.

Will felt a buzz in his stomach. 'I can hear it all in my head. The overdubs, the harmonies, the keyboards.'

'Keyboards?'

'Yeah, my sister has a Casio. It's wank, but if we put it through an FX pedal or something it could be interesting.'

'All right, Jean-Michel Jarre.' Jake smiled.

'I can't wait for Amy to hear it!' said Will.

'Oooh, Amy this, Amy that.'

'It's the first time I've mentioned her!' Will squealed.

Luke stood up from the kit, stretching out his arms. 'We can send it to venues all over the place once it's done. We aren't going to get noticed in Malford.'

An hour later, the session stuttered to an end, the boys skinned up and packed up their gear, chattering away woozily about launch parties, radio play and video locations. At that moment, everything seemed possible; realism was an unwanted guest.

*

Will sat cross-legged on Jake's bedroom floor; the night was drawing in and next door's kids were making the most of the last bit of light in the garden, squawking with delight as they pelted water balloons at each other. Jake's room was sparse: a small portable television, an old transistor radio, dog-eared copies of *FHM* and a scattering of books he'd surely never read. Jake strummed away badly on an acoustic, before giving up and laying it across his lap.

'Say thanks to your dad for me,' said Will in a tired croak.

'It's all right, it's been good for him to have something to focus on since Mum left.'

Will looked at him for a moment. 'Did you ever work out what happened there?'

'I dunno really. He was working away a lot, they were rowing all the time...' His voice wavered. 'I've invited her to come see us play a few times, but nothing.' Jake's eyes begin to fill with tears; he looked away as he continued to speak. Will had never seen him cry before; he fidgeted with his shoelace, wrapping it tightly around his finger, pretending not to notice.

'Her new fella's got a couple of kids of his own.'

'You'll always be her son,' said Will, embarrassed by the mawkish sentiments.

There was an awkward beat. 'It doesn't feel like it right now,' said Jake. He shook his head, like a dog at the beach shaking off the salty seawater. 'Here, have another beer,' he said, passing Will a stubby.

'No, thanks, I better get going. But if you ever want to talk...'

Jake wiped his eyes with the sleeve of his hoodie.

'I'm OK. Promise.'

*

Amy plonked two Malibu and Cokes down on the table for her and Charlotte. With a full face of makeup and a hint of cleavage, she'd never had trouble getting served in town. The Griffin was dead; a man with tobacco-stained fingers sat at the bar talking to anyone who unwittingly made eye contact and offering out unsolicited fruit machine advice.

'So, how's it going with Will then?' asked Charlotte.

'He's really sweet...'

'But...'

'But nothing.' Amy laughed. 'He's shy, but I like that. Better than the arrogant pricks who usually hit on me.'

Charlotte took a long slug of her drink and eyed Amy. 'You're not falling for him, are you?'

Amy blushed and washed a fizz of Malibu and Coke around her mouth. 'He'll see me through to university,' she replied, though she could see from Charlotte's face that she didn't believe a word of it. 'How's it going with Jake?'

'Good. I mean we don't hang out that much, but when we do, the sex is electric.'

A brief image of the two of them shagging flickered in her mind, she shook it away like a Etch a Sketch.

'How is it with Will?' Charlotte winked.

'We haven't gone that far yet.'

'Why? He a virgin?'

'Christ, you think?'

'Fuck no, he's in a band, he's probably riddled with STDs.'

Charlotte cackled and reached into her handbag. She pulled out her lip gloss and reapplied it, smudging her lips together to smooth it out.

They ordered another drink and bitched away about girls from school: Zara Parker was already pregnant, and Tina Hope was now working full-time in the Co-Op. Two guys playing pool in paint-splattered work clothes sporadically looked their way. The girls ignored their less-than-subtle glances and carried on chatting.

'Fancy a game of doubles?' asked one of them, gelled blonde curtains and prematurely yellow teeth.

'We're good, thanks,' Charlotte replied, shooting Amy a 'kill me now' look.

He moved in closer; she could smell the cigarettes on his breath now. 'Come on, one on each team. We'll teach you how to play.'

'Ha, don't flatter yourself,' said Charlotte pointedly.

'Alright, darlin', cheer up,' he spat.

Charlotte rolled her eyes and turned back around to face Amy.

'You'd be really pretty if you smiled, you know that.'

Charlotte's chair screeched across the wooden floor as she stood up to meet them. 'Look, you desperate prick, don't tell us how to spend our evening, alright?'

'Woah, calm down, love.' He raised both hands out in front of him palms first, racking his brain for a comeback that didn't come.

'Come on, Amy, we're going,' said Charlotte, necking her drink before grabbing her by the wrist and fleeing the pub.

*

Will dumped his guitar on the brown formica kitchen table, amongst the circular letters and unpaid bills.

'Hi, love, how was practice?' Helen called out. Will traipsed through to the living room. She was sat on the sofa with a large glass of white wine. The television was on, but she was staring straight through it. She turned the volume down with the remote. Will eyed the drink in her hand. 'It was good. We worked on a new song which sounded awesome. We're gonna record it.'

Helen caught his look and put her glass down with a clatter on the table.

'That's great. Your dad would be so proud, you know.'

Will winced; he could tell from the inflection in her voice that she was already half-cut. He knew that she meant well, but he found all the tugging on the heartstrings exhausting. It had been almost two years since his father had died and she was clearly still some way off accepting it. In the first few months, she had rarely managed to drag herself out of bed, and that was when Will had locked himself away in his room and played the guitar until the skin on his fingertips went hard, attempting to paint over the crushing sadness he felt. She'd lost her job as a nurse, and was now a receptionist at the opticians, when she managed to make it in. He was terrified she was going to lose this one too, then where would they be?

'Well, he's never going to hear it, is he, Mum?'

She rocked her head back and forth gently. 'He will, he will.'

Will said nothing. The spiritual stuff his mum believed in meant nothing to him, but her feelings did. He forced a tiny smile and looked away. He thought that he should probably hug her but couldn't bring himself to. He climbed the stairs, guitar case in one hand, bowl of leftover Bolognese balancing in the other.

'Izzy, can we borrow your keyboard when we record?' he shouted towards his sister's room.

'No!'

'Thanks!'

He half-unlaced his shoes and kicked them off across the room. The light from his bedside lamp was dim; tattered posters, souvenir ticket stubs and pilfered setlists plastered the walls, hanging there resolute. He changed into a pair of shorts and the old PE shirt he wore as pyjamas, sat on the bed and began to shovel the food into his mouth with a fork. It was deadly quiet in the house and he could hear his ears buzz, like there was a wasp trapped inside them he couldn't shake out. Jake's father, Mick, had given them some earplugs to wear, but none of them like the muffled sound and the feeling of being underwater. He thought about Amy, when he could see her again, and wondered if she was thinking about him right now too. He turned on the television and flicked through the channels. *Panorama*, snooker, *A Touch of Frost* and some show about trainee lawyers living together. He switched it off and lay back on the bed. His mind wandered back to the time his dad had taken him to a football match when he was young. He couldn't remember much about the game, just that the stadium was awash with the scent of Deep Heat and cigars, and that the roar from the crowd was so loud his dad had to cover his little ears with his hands when a goal was scored. He shut his eyes and fell asleep.

CHAPTER 8

Will pranced around his room in a towel, thrashing his limbs about to the sound of The Prodigy. He squirted some deodorant under his arms and spiked his wet hair up in a mohawk, before swiftly returning it to normality. Amy's parents were out for the evening at some line-dancing event at the community centre and she had invited him over. He knew what that meant and his jittery mind had been unable to concentrate on anything else all day. It would be his first time, but he was certain it wouldn't be Amy's. He let his towel drop to the floor and checked himself in the mirror. He wondered if he was big enough, hairy enough, and if that's what testicles were meant to look like.

Helen, under the illusion that Amy's parents would be there, and that he couldn't go empty-handed, dug out a cheap bottle of wine from the larder. He snatched it from her with clammy palms, his stomach doing Fosburys as he laced up his shoes and left the house. He strode purposely through the streets in a racing green T-shirt, grey hoodie and baggy jeans, muddy and fraying at the bottom. He swung by Blockbusters on the way. The air-conditioning hummed lowly as he browsed the racks – *Braveheart, Toy Story, GoldenEye* – the choice felt irrelevant; he knew they wouldn't get more than ten minutes into it. He finally settled upon *Waterworld*, which somehow he still hadn't seen.

As he approached Amy's house, he steadied himself. Everything seemed so much larger, and more pristine, than his. The hall light smudged in the frosted glass as he puffed out his cheeks and knocked on the door three times in a way that he hoped that Amy would know it was him. In the few seconds it took her to answer, he changed pose multiple times, deciding that bottle under one arm and video in the other hand looked most casual.

'Welcome to Chateau Stevens. Come on in,' said Amy theatrically.

'I brought wine,' said Will, thrusting out the bottle.

Amy surveyed the label. 'Chardonnay – classy.'

'Is it? It's my mum's. Sorry if it's rubbish. I don't think she's too fussy at the moment.'

Amy smiled from the corner of her mouth, gestured him into the house and shut the door behind him. 'Have you eaten? There's some leftover stir-fry if you want some.'

'I'm good, I had shepherd's pie,' replied Will, moving through the hall behind her.

Amy pulled a corkscrew out from the kitchen drawer. 'Did you know that the only difference between shepherd's pie and cottage pie is that one is made with lamb and the other with beef?'

'Never really thought about it.'

'It's like pasta – there's like a million different names for the different shapes of it, but it's all just pasta, isn't it?'

'Yeah, it's like the difference between 2B and HB pencils – they're all just pencils, aren't they?' said Will, feeling obliged to join in.

Amy laughed and brushed her hand down Will's chest. A buzz of anticipation permeated through him. He kissed her gently on the forehead and smiled gawkily. Amy poured them a sloppy glass of wine each and revelled in showing Will around the house. Dressed in a tight white Pulp T-shirt, faded denim miniskirt, she cruised effortlessly barefoot across the carpet.

The tour of the house stopped abruptly in Amy's bedroom. Piles of clothes and magazines scattered on the floor. Kurt Cobain loomed down on them from a poster on the wall, his blond hair and blue eyes vivid even in black and white. Will breathed in the scent of her perfume in the air, like Amy but magnified. She slipped a CD into the stereo. It was something guitary that Will didn't recognise. He stopped himself from asking what it was. Amy's bed was small, with a dark mahogany frame and springy violet mattress. They sat down side by side on it and he kissed her boldly, without words, her lips sumptuous as he pressed his against them. She took his hand and placed it on her chest; he slipped his hand up through her top and into her white cotton bra.

'Is this OK?' he asked. Amy nodded. She slid her skirt off. He put his hand between her thighs; it felt warm and wet as he grazed his fingers back and forth.

'Are you going to take your clothes off, Will?' She laughed.

Will nodded and pulled clumsily at his tee, panicking momentarily as his head got stuck, before yanking it roughly over his ears and kissing her again. Amy unhooked her bra and let it drop to the floor. Will looked at her bare breasts for the first time. He quickly decided that they were the greatest thing he'd ever seen, and he couldn't believe he was allowed to touch them.

'Have you got any protection?' whispered Amy.

Will pulled a small blue and silver packet out from his trouser pocket; it felt cold and smooth between his damp fingers.

'Presumptuous.' Amy giggled.

Will struggled with the johnny for what felt like an age, before finally managing to roll it over himself. He kissed the inside of her thighs, before fumbling to slide it in. It felt like every synapse was on fire, as he thrust in and out, jerkily at first, before finding a rhythm. Amy, clinging to his clammy shoulders, kissed his neck and he felt like he would cum just from that. He wondered how long he had to hold on for before it was no longer considered premature and felt he just about stumbled over the line as he finished with a self-conscious grunt. They lay in a sweaty, naked embrace on top of the sheets. In the light of her little bedside lamp, Will felt decidedly sober and exposed, but a warm afterglow flowed gently through him, as if his entire life to date had culminated in that moment. They lay there, a comfortable silence drifting between them. Amy pierced it with a question.

'What are you doing next year, Will?'

'How'd you mean?'

'I mean, like uni or whatever?'

'We've all decided we are going to defer for a year. Give the band a go. You?'

Amy fidgeted with the edge of the bedsheet, tracing her finger along the seam. 'I've applied for English Lit at a few places. I want to go to London, really, but King's is hard to get into.'

Will felt a pang of sadness. He knew that she would get in. He thought that she could probably do anything that she set her mind to.

'Does your mum mind you not going to university?' Amy probed tentatively.

'Not really. Nobody in my family ever has. I don't think she's even noticed I've finished college, to be honest.'

'My dad's always on my case about my grades. Does my head in.'

There was an awkward pause.

'I'm sorry, that's insensitive. I should be glad he's still around, I guess.'

'It's OK,' said Will.

'Do you miss him?'

Will steadily composed an answer in his head. 'I never really got to know him properly, to be honest. I was too young.'

Amy gazed at him and nodded slowly.

'I just feel sad that I didn't spend more time with him. He was always asking me to go fishing with him, or take stuff to the tip together, but I just wasn't interested.' He shivered. Amy kissed his lips and pulled the sheets up over them.

'I better get going soon,' said Will.

Amy snuggled into him even tighter. 'Just ten minutes more.'

*

The next day, Will sat on his bed, cradling his acoustic. He picked the strings loosely with his fingers, noodling around in minor chords – the melancholy tone at odds with how he was feeling for once. He grabbed a notepad from his drawer; it was peppered with doodles of SharpShooter logos, angsty slogans and trial runs of his autograph – just in case they ever had to do an HMV signing session at short notice. He wrote the title 'Lost Together' on a blank page, but no more words came.

Helen, who was seemingly having one of her better days, knocked on the door and softly pushed it ajar, her hair greying at the roots and pale yellow T-shirt loose-fitting.

'Dinner's ready, love.'

'Coming.'

He carried on playing the guitar for a moment more, before hopping up and joining her and Izzy downstairs at the table.

'What is it, Mum?' asked Izzy, her face young and not yet fully formed, like a caricature of a girl.

'Lasagne. Make sure you take some salad too, please,' she said to them both. 'How was last night, Will?'

'Fine,' he grunted. *If only you knew.*

'Will's got a girlfriend! Will's got a girlfriend!' chanted Izzy.

'Shhh, you,' said Helen, putting her finger to her lips. 'You should invite her around here sometime.'

Will felt his ears get warm; he scratched at the back of his head with his fingernails. He couldn't bring Amy over: the house was too much of a state and his mum was far too unpredictable to make such plans.

'Maybe,' he said eventually.

After dinner, he tried to read in his room, but he couldn't shake Amy from his mind. Visceral images of the night before made it impossible to concentrate on the page, so he decided to make her a mixtape instead.

He pulled a clutch of CDs down from the rack and sorted hastily through them on the bed. His music collection was growing exponentially and meant everything to him. He loved sifting through the records at Tony's, and all the money he could beg, steal and borrow was spent on getting the latest releases. They provided the tiny hits of serotonin he needed to get by. When his dad had died, he'd clung to certain songs like a life raft, so much so that he could no longer listen to them. He pushed a new cassette in, pressed play on the CD deck and jammed the play and record buttons down together on the tape machine.

He chose some of his favourite songs ('Enjoy the Silence', 'This Charming Man' and 'Say It Ain't So'), some songs he knew Amy liked ('Lithium', 'The Universal', 'Basket Case') and some new bands he thought she might not have heard of (The Breeders, Kenickie and Mansun), making sure that the lyrics weren't too sappy or said too much.

An hour later, he rewound the cassette, took it out and slipped it into the case. In childlike bubble-writing he scrawled what he hoped was a suitably romantic and mysterious title – *Fragments of Youth* – on it and stashed it in his bag.

CHAPTER 9

It was a hazy summer's morning and the estate was awash with activity. Pete pulled up outside the house and rasped his horn. Will was sitting upright on the couch, shoes on, guitar by his side, ready.

'I'm off,' he shouted up the stairs to Helen, who was yet to rise.

SoundScene studios was a converted barn on the outskirts of town, owned by a grizzly muso called Kev who had played bass in various bands in the '80s. He introduced himself and helped them load their ramshackle gear into the live room. The boys peered longingly through the glass at the mixing desk. It was as wide as the room, with so many buttons they wondered what they could all be for. Tony arrived shortly after with £300 cash in a brown envelope, enough to buy them two days to record, mix and master two songs.

'You guys set up in here, and the drums round there,' said Kev in an indistinguishable northern accent, issuing them each a pair of battered over-ear headphones.

'Are you sticking around, Tony?' asked Will.

'Of course.' He smiled, baring uneven, yellow teeth. He turned to Kev. 'Make sure you capture what these boys have got live.'

Kev nodded. 'I'll get the drums and bass from the live takes and we'll then re-do the guitars and vocals, and any overdubs.'

After a few warm-up takes, the gang slowly got into their stride, Tony watching dotingly through the glass, waving his hands around as if he was conducting an orchestra. Will homed in on the fretboard and counted the bars in his head to make sure everything was the right length. He lowered his head and tried to steady his hands, as if he was playing a game of *Operation* and one false move would send alarms ringing and they'd have to start again. It struck him that these would be the definitive versions of the songs they played live, and although that meant nothing to the outside world, to him it was huge. Luke gripped the drumsticks so tightly he could feel blood blisters forming in his fleshy palms. He pushed through the discomfort and pounded away, fighting the urge to overdo the rolls and fills.

After a couple of hours, they had satisfactory takes of both songs. Luke and Jake made a rancid Pot Noodle each, stinking out the control room, and watched the graphic equalisers dance as Pete laid down his bass tracks. He sat rigid on a stool with his skinny arms wrapped around the body of the guitar, his fingers leaping decisively along the fretboard. He chanced a couple of flourishes he'd not been brave enough to do live and the others smiled at each other in the control room. Will was next. His mouth was salty dry and throat tightening as he added his lead parts, cranking up the delay and reverb and filling out the spaces with broad swashes of colour. Tony, whose gentle presence helped to reassure him, hummed out some extra guitar lines he could hear in his head and Will did his best to assimilate them with his guitar, thickening out the collage of sound.

By the time Jake got into the vocal booth, he was a caged animal. He sang melodically and resolutely, contrasting the wailing vibrato with tiny sparks of guttural angst.

'*I've been walking in the morning rain, thinking of you. It's not a matter of life or death, this shit that we do,*' he growled into the microphone. He cupped the headphones with his hands and swayed his head as if he was in Band Aid, the other lads taking the piss through the glass and Tony giving him a thumbs-up or thumbs-down with each take.

Kev managed to make Izzy's Casio sound more Kraftwerk, and less 'Tomy's My First Keyboard', as Will added some one-fingered counter-melodies, elevating the songs to new levels.

Six pm soon rolled around and the first session wound to an end. The guys fizzed with excitement in the car park, the tunes spiralling around their heads.

'It's sounding ace, guys,' said Tony.

'You were loving it, Tone, getting right involved.' Luke laughed.

'Yeah, always fancied being a producer, studied music at college, ended up running a record store instead,' he sighed.

'And a fine establishment it is too,' said Jake, patting him on the back.

'I can't make it tomorrow, I've gotta take care of the store, but just focus – see through what you've started.'

'We will, promise,' replied Will, with an acute sense of responsibility.

'I can't afford to give you another bash at it, that's for sure!' Tony laughed, getting into his red Mini Cooper. 'Let me have the master when you've got it. I can't wait to hear it, boys.'

The next day, the boys stood in the control room, anxiously listening to the previous day's work with fresh ears, a hint of the outside world shimmering through the skylight. The tracks sounded raw and vital as they boomed out of the giant speakers. They shot each other satisfied glances.

In the vocal booth, Will warbled along with Jake a cappella to warm his voice up. Kev pressed record, and Will focused hard, doubling up on alternate verse lines and choruses. Some of the notes were unreachably high, so Jake did them instead – their little secret. When it came to mixing, Kev wittered on about EQs and compression, and none of the band wanted to be the one who asked what any of it meant. He shook his head at the possibility of making the guitar, bass, vocals and the drums all louder.

'If I make them all louder, then nothing is louder,' he explained in dulcet tones. They understood what he meant but wanted it anyway.

'The instruments are fine,' said Jake. 'Just turn the vocals up a bit. They need to cut through on the radio.' He grinned.

Will gleefully wrote 'SharpShooter – The Outsiders' on the freshly burnt CD with a marker pen and slipped it into its little plastic wallet.

On the ride home, they passed around a spliff and listened to the songs three times over. Tepid summer rain lashed against the window; Will leant his head against it, feeling safe and warm, cocooned inside the car, listening to something special the four of them had created. Even as it was happening, he knew that he would one day be nostalgic for this moment.

CHAPTER 10

Helen carefully folded a pile of white paper napkins. She filled two large bowls with crisps and poured herself a plastic cup of wine.

'Steady on, Mum, the guests haven't even arrived yet,' Will hissed.

She put the cup down on the table and emptied an industrial-sized packet of peanuts into several polystyrene bowls. 'Do you think we've got enough food?'

Will scanned the epic buffet and nodded.

In the corner of the hall, the DJ strained to set up his rickety decks and a set of disco-lights on a thinly disguised wallpapering table.

'So, I finally get to meet the mythical Amy this evening?'

Will stifled a blush. 'I guess so.'

On the community centre walls, among the flyers for aerobics lessons and ante-natal classes, were hastily printed pictures of Will in the bath as a baby, as a toddler feeding some chickens, and on the beach in Cornwall with his grandad. Shiny metallic 'Happy 18th' balloons were fastened to each table, trying their best to escape.

'How many people are we expecting?'

'About twenty or so family. And all your friends. You did invite them, didn't you?'

'Yes, Mum,' replied Will, rolling his eyes, though in truth he'd been so non-committal about it all, he wasn't sure how many would turn up. The DJ played a blast of M People's 'Moving on Up' to test the sound system and Will hoped that it wasn't a sign of things to come.

Elderly relatives began to arrive in clusters. Will glanced anxiously at the door, hoping that Amy or Pete, or someone, would turn up and save him from the cyclical small talk. Helen scurried around the hall, topping up drinks and wiping down tables with blue roll, smiling sympathetically at Will whenever she caught his eye. The DJ clumsily transitioned between Ace of Base and Right Said Fred and Will exhaled deeply.

Eventually, the door opened, letting in a blast of summer air, and Jake, Luke, Pete, Amy and Charlotte bounded through together, as if they'd all been waiting outside just to test him. Will gave Amy a warm but self-conscious hug, and they kissed, their lips barely touching.

'Happy birthday,' said Jake, punching him slightly too hard on the shoulder. His eyes were bloodshot and veiny, and his clothing reeked of smoke. 'I bumped into the Fletch and his mates on the way – they said they might pop in later.'

'Great,' said Will, trying to mask his indifference. Fletch lived on the estate; he was one of those kids who looked ancient but was actually just a couple of years above them at school. With his receding hair and bum-fluff chin hair, his physical appearance had peaked in Year Ten. He and his crew were the type who had made it their mission at school to break supply teachers, and could be found drinking White Lightning in the park, despite now being old enough to drink in pubs.

Charlotte, buoyed by the hip flask of vodka in her handbag, strode purposefully around the hall meeting and greeting Will's friends, enjoying the knowledge that each and every one of them would want her. Amy tagged along a few yards behind – Tails to her Sonic.

'Amy – come and meet my mum,' said Will, taking her by the hand over to the adults' table.

Helen stood up, smiling widely. 'Ah, you must be Amy?'

'Yes, pleasure to meet you.'

Will enjoyed how formal they were being with each other.

'It's good to meet you at last. Izzy and I were beginning to think you weren't real.'

Will squirmed, running his fingers across the bridge of his nose. *Do mums subscribe to a catalogue of embarrassing things to say?*

Izzy came bounding across the dancefloor, a pink bow in her hair and white party dress already showing signs of sliding around on the dusty wooden floor; she looked up at Amy. 'She is real!' she squealed with a sense of wonderment.

'I am.' Amy laughed.

'And you're pretty.'

'Why, thank you,' said Amy, owning it.

'That's enough flattery, thanks, Izzy,' said Will, tickling her under the arms.

71

The hall filled up further, the DJ ploughed shamelessly through a Smash Hits compilation, ignoring the requests he'd been given. Some danced tentatively, while others sat eating mini sausage rolls and triangular sandwiches from paper plates. Outside, a spontaneous game of football had broken out on the lawn with a partially inflated Mitre. Jake juggled the ball from his left foot to his right, spilling his beer as he did so, screaming 'Gascoigne,' as he spanked it against the brick wall. Luke watched the ball come off the wall, flicked it up and headed it, a move he instantly regretted when it left a wet, muddy imprint on his forehead. The low light outside made the ball difficult to judge and Will felt useless in front of Amy and Charlotte as the ball spooned off his shins.

A little after 9.30pm, Fletch and a couple of other guys, known for shifting gear and hotwiring cars on the estate, rocked up. Will introduced them to the girls out of a sense of polite obligation before heading inside to check on the party. Auntie Eve broke away from the 'Macarena' to make suitable noises about what a lovely girl Amy was, and his nan kissed him on the cheek and said she was off home 'to get the curtains drawn'. Will headed to the bar to buy his first legal pint. It felt wrong to be buying his own drink on his birthday, but the new-found legality of it evened things out.

David, a boy he went to school with, approached from behind, tapping him on the shoulder. 'I saw your photo in *The Herald* the other day – all in big coats, looking moody.'

'Yeah, gotta look the part.' Will smiled.

'Just don't forget us all when you're famous, will you?'

Forget him? He could barely remember his name now. Will's head felt floaty as he joined Pete on the dancefloor, dancing inanely to the drivel that was playing. They successfully harangued the DJ into playing some Oasis and strutted around the dancefloor in the simian gait of the Gallagher brothers.

Outside on the lawn, Fletch was in the ear of Amy. Speaking at her and turning his head away every so often to spit on the grass.

'Is Will your boyfriend then?'

'Yes, I guess so,' said Amy, unsure of the line of questioning.

'He's absolutely punching, you know that?'

Amy tried to fight a blush and took a swig of her Smirnoff Ice, warm and saccharine.

'He's a bit wet, isn't he? I remember at school he dropped his plate in the canteen and almost cried.'

'Is that the best you can do?' Amy laughed.

Fletch grinned, revealing a missing front tooth as he did so. 'You've got a cracking rack, and it's a shame it's wasted on him, is all I'm saying.' He knew he was pushing his luck now. Amy scowled, said nothing and headed inside to find Will.

With Amy out of the way, Jake and Charlotte sidled up beside Fletch.

'You bring the gear?' asked Jake, through gritted teeth.

'Yeah, you got the money?'

'Of course,' said Jake, handing over a scrunch of notes from his pay packet. Fletch pressed a baggie into his hand and in one swift movement Jake dropped it into the pocket of his beige combat trousers.

Back inside, 'Not in Love' gently radiated from the speakers and the couples rocked slowly from foot to foot.

Amy nestled her head in the nook of Will's shoulder. He looked across the room and saw Luke snogging his cousin Laura up against the wall; he did some quick mental arithmetic and was relieved to find she was sixteen, just. Her eyes were closed, but Luke's were open, and he flashed a mortifying wink at Will, who looked away with disdain. Jake, chewing at the inside of his cheek, stood on the edge of the dancefloor, Charlotte clinging to him, skinny and wasted.

Helen, her face flushed deep red and unsteady on her heels, asked the DJ to cut the music so she could say a few words. She clutched the microphone tightly in her fist, a piercing squeal of feedback rang out.

'Testing, testing, is this thing on?' she slurred. Will winced, bracing himself as the murmuring stopped and all eyes were on her.

'I just want to say thank you to everyone for coming,' she said, leading the crowd in an off-key rendition of 'Happy Birthday'. As it dissolved to an end, she gave a blurry smile before leaning backwards on the DJ's table, falling straight through it. The crowd gasped. Guffaws of laughter spread like wildfire throughout the hall. Will stood motionless, head cradled in his hands. Jake stepped forward and helped her to her feet. Helen dusted herself off and walked towards Will, a deep sadness in her eyes.

'Couldn't you have kept it together just for one night?'

'Oh, Will, lighten up, will you? It's a party.' She shrugged.

'You're a joke, Mum,' he spat. Hot tears stung his eyes as he flounced off out the door, through the gate towards the main road.

Amy scurried after him.

74

'What's he pissed off about? It was hilarious!' Fletch laughed. Jake shot him a death stare and he instantly backed down.

Amy, now feeling the full effects of the alcohol outside in the cool dark air, searched the surrounding area. She hotfooted it over a ditch full of stinging nettles and into the small woodland area opposite, peering through a tangle of rotten branches and calling out Will's name. She levered open the rusty iron gates at the end of the woods and found him in the graveyard, slumped against a headstone, sobbing into his sleeve. She glanced at the face of it – John William Green, 1949–1995 – the epitaph obscured by Will's prone body.

'Will, it's me,' she said softly.

He lifted his head up slowly as she perched herself down beside him.

'Come on, they are all waiting for you back inside.'

Will shook his head. 'Is everyone still laughing at her?'

'No. Come on. It's not that bad. It could have happened to anyone.'

He swiped at a tear under his eye as if shooing away a fly. 'It's not just that, though, is it? I'm the one helping Izzy with her homework, making sure she's got her lunch money and brushed her teeth.'

'I know, and you're doing a great job,' she said, taking his hand.

'It's exhausting, though,' he said, looking at her. 'I'm making sure she doesn't fall apart, but who's looking out for me?'

'You've got me,' she said gently. 'We've got each other.'

Will flashed a wry smile and gazed at her for a moment, the goosebumped-skin of her exposed arms shimmering in the moonlight.

'I love you, Amy… is that OK?'

There was a momentary pause in which his heart felt like an elevator freefalling.

'Of course it is,' she whispered. 'I love you too.'

CHAPTER 11

The Rugby Club stage creaked under the weight of bodies and equipment. A Union Jack hung stoically on the wall and particles of dust glittered in the stage lights. The hypnotic groove of 'Vital Signs' gyrated to an end and Will looked out at the audience: a more than healthy turn-out for a rainy Wednesday night. Among the throng of kids in homemade SharpShooter T-shirts and deep-pocket jeans were Amy, Charlotte, Helen, Mick and Tony (simultaneously doing the lights and sound); all the people he cared most about in the world. He ripped into the final chord and placed his guitar against his amp for maximum feedback, as stinging applause rang out from the boisterous crowd.

'Did you get it all?' said Jake, bounding off the stage, breathing heavily.

'Sure did,' said Mick, excitedly stowing the camcorder back in its case. 'Might be a bit shaky though, the bass was rattling my knees!'

Jake patted him on the back and wiped his sweaty brow with his sleeve.

'I reckon you've got this in the bag!' said Mick.

'Calm down, Dad, it's only a Battle of the Bands,' said Jake nonchalantly.

The gang stood against the back wall together chewing the fat. Will took hold of Amy's hand and held it tightly, creating a vacuum between their clammy palms. Luke made an unsuccessful attempt to chirps a goth-looking girl in an oversized Korn T-shirt while Helen and Mick made polite small talk, struggling to hear each other over the final band, Paper Soul. Will watched them for a moment, the tiny, forced gestures and polite pleasantries between them, before Pete snapped him out of it.

'Your mum hasn't come to a gig in ages.'

'Yeah, she's promised she's not going to embarrass herself this time.' He smiled ruefully.

Jake, hand on the small of Charlotte's back, turned his head towards her and they kissed sloppily with tongues, devouring each other's faces. Will could see members of opposing band The Blisters giving them daggers, their jealousy thinly concealed. In their mid-twenties, the trio's faux-punk set had opened proceedings and gone down well. They had been steadily getting wasted in the corner since.

'You look hot tonight, Ames,' shouted Charlotte on the music. Amy smiled, her hair glistening in the kaleidoscope of lights. She twirled self-consciously on the spot and took a glug of her drink. Will could see that Charlotte's approval still meant so much to her, as shallow as her comments were.

Charlotte turned back to Jake and clung to him tightly, his black T-shirt soaked with warm sweat.

'You got anything?' she whispered in his ear.

'Yeah, but later – not with my dad around.'

Will looked on disapprovingly. He could tell what they were discussing and it seemed a bit excessive for a Wednesday night. But it also irritated him that he and Amy weren't at least offered some, as if they were fusty squares compared to him and Charlotte.

Paper Soul stumbled away – the wiry singer struggling to make himself heard over a guitarist and keyboardist seemingly playing in different keys to each other. Oblivious to the weediness of his voice, he strutted around trying to work the apathetic crowd, some of which were now sitting cross-legged on the floor.

Tony, in a faded Swervedriver T-shirt, came back from the bar with another tray of pints for everyone.

'Cheers, Tone. What did you think of the set?' asked Will.

'You need to tighten up on the changes a bit and watch your timings going into the choruses. Don't worry, I made you sound shit-hot, though.'

'There's no pleasing some people.' Jake winked.

'You can get away with a bit of sloppiness here, but not when you hit the big smoke.'

Will's insides smiled at the prospect of playing London. 'How's it going with the single?' he asked.

'Yeah, good, I've nearly finished the artwork. I say we launch it at the shop weekend after next?'

'Sure thing,' said Pete.

Paper Soul's cod reggae final number ended and the venue descended into a myriad of murmurs. The bubbling noise was interrupted by a man in a white suit stepping up on the stage. He ignored the childish heckles thrown in his direction, tapped the microphone and cleared his throat.

'Thank you all for coming out this evening. It's been a tough decision for the judges, but the results are, in third place – Bruised Fruit.'

A group of gawky kids in matching Hawaiian shirts high-fived, happy with their lot.

'In second place – The Blisters.'

There were dissenting grumbles from the corner as they awaited the winner.

'And after careful consideration, the winner of our fifth annual Battle of the Bands, and of the £150 equipment voucher, is… drum roll… SharpShooter!'

The boys pumped their fists and let out a collective 'yes'. The sibilance of the 'S' hissing across the high-ceiling room as their drinks flew everywhere.

The Blisters booed in unison in almost comic fashion. 'Fix,' shouted the curly-haired singer, decked out in a stonewash denim jacket with Stiff Little Fingers and The Damned badges stitched on it.

'Not fair, they had their own soundman, and lights,' said his skinhead mate, once the applause had died down.

Jake smirked, angering them more. He dodged a barrage of cans as they climbed on stage to collect their prize, bobbing and weaving mockingly as he took the envelope from the compere and they posed for a shot for the local paper.

'Speech!' shouted Mick. Jake, half-cut by now, grinned and flipped him the bird.

'Oi, watch it,' hollered Mick.

Helen, gushing with pride, engulfed Will in a big congratulatory hug as he came off stage. He couldn't smell alcohol on her for once and hoped that the incident at his party had brought her drinking to a head, although he wouldn't have banked on it. Uneasy that the other bands were watching, he shook her off and headed to the toilet. He pushed through the splintering wooden door. The white tiled floor was awash with filthy water and mushy tissues. The stench of waste choked his nostrils.

Under the fluorescent light of the bogs, he felt less sober, less in control. He stared at himself in the mirror, bedraggled and sweaty. He slid the palm of his hand down it, as if he could remove himself from it. He hated using the urinals, but the only cubical was engaged. He stood there, desperate for a slash, but couldn't go. He shut his eyes and eventually it flowed. Just as it did, in crashed two of The Blisters; the surprise jolted him, making him spray warm piss on his jeans. He finished up hastily and zipped up his flies.

'Who did your mum gobble off for that result?' snorted the curly-haired one.

'Fuck off.'

'You guys think you're so good,' said Skinhead with bile.

'We won fair and square,' said Will, turning to leave. As he did so, the pair leapt in front of him, blocking the exit, a drunken wildness in their eyes. Will grappled with them, trying to escape. He clawed at Skinhead's shirt but couldn't get any purchase to move him. Hearing the commotion, Jake burst out of the cubicle.

'What's going on here, eh?' he said, staring them down.

'Oh, here he is – Mick Jagger,' said Curly.

Jake lodged himself in between the duo and Will, feeling invincible. Charlotte sheepishly emerged from the cubicle, discreetly wiping her nose with the back of her hand.

'Calm down, lads, it's not our fault you lost to a bunch of teenagers.'

Will laughed, a scornful laugh that surprised himself. Charlotte, like a baby giraffe taking its first steps, tip-toed across the room in her heels and leant on the sink for support.

'What you doing in the men's? You skank,' spat Curly with real vitriol.

'Fuck off!' Jake frothed. 'Get out of here before I lose it!'

The pair laughed dismissively and headed back into the venue as Will and Charlotte tried to hold Jake back.

'It's not worth it,' Charlotte pleaded. 'Your dad's in there, he doesn't want to see you fighting.'

Jake, silently seething, tried to free himself from Will's grasp.

'She's right,' said Will. 'We might lose our prize too if it all kicks off.'

Jake could see the genuine concern in their eyes and began to calm. His breathing slowly returning to normal, he straightened his T-shirt and ran his hands through his greasy black fringe, trying to compose himself.

Charlotte took his hand and they headed back into the venue.

'Where have you all been?' said Amy, as they emerged.

'There was an incident in the toilets, doesn't matter,' said Charlotte.

Amy looked at her, weary and fazed, for once, and decided not to press for details.

'Everyone else shot off. I had to start reading my book I was so bored.'

'Only you would bring a book to a gig.' Charlotte smiled.

The music stopped dead and the house lights came up. Amy squinted her eyes from the glare and took hold of her friend's arm. 'Let's get out of here.'

The boys loaded their gear out of the venue and sat hotboxing in the car park, laughing uncontrollably.

'Did you see Curly's face when we won? I thought the little twat was going to explode,' said Pete, blowing out grey smoke.

Jake took a toke and craned his head to the back seat. 'You boys were on fire tonight. I know I'm wasted, but I mean it.'

Will grinned. 'Thanks for saving me from those pricks.'

'It's OK. No one picks on my best mate,' said Jake woozily. 'Besides, I thought you were a bit old to still be getting bog-washed.'

Will stuck his middle finger up at him and took a drag of the spliff.

Pete turned to Luke. 'The last song – you kept on banging away, I thought you were never going to finish.'

Luke looked at him for a split second. 'That's what your mum said.'

The boys guffawed as Pete started the engine to head back to the estate.

Back on The Grantham, Will said goodnight to the others with jubilant hugs. But noticed Jake linger as he headed up the driveway.

'You wanna come in? Kip over like you used to,' asked Will.

'Sure,' said Jake, following him.

Will laid out the little red airbed and Jake worked the wheezy foot pump until it filled with air. He collapsed down on it in a haze and pulled a blanket over him. Will put Teenage Fanclub on the stereo quietly and they lay staring up at the ceiling, talking about the evening's events, illuminated by the bedside lamp.

'How's everything going with Amy?' asked Jake, turning on his side.

'She's great,' said Will, still feeling the dizzying effects of all the drink. 'She really is.'

'I'm so happy for you, mate,' said Jake softly.

'Cheers,' mouthed Will, but no sound came out.

'I know you've had a rough couple of years with your dad and everything.'

'It's OK...'

'No, if anyone deserves some happiness, it's you.'

Will squirmed at how open he was being. 'You were the only one who was there for me through that. I won't forget that,' he said eventually.

He wrapped the duvet around himself tightly.

'I just want this.'

'What?' asked Jake.

'You, me, the band. Everything, forever,' Will replied, turning off the lamp.

CHAPTER 12

Amy and Will sat on the train, their hands clasped together, watching the green and yellow fields roll past. They shared a can of beer, their faces basking in the swollen summer sun. Jake and Charlotte sat in the chairs opposite, groggy from the gig the night before. They were all heading to the south coast for the weekend. Charlotte's family had a holiday home down there. This was the first year she was allowed to use it alone, and the others had jumped at the chance to get out of Malford for a couple of days.

Set back from the beach, the place was bright and spacious, the smell of last summer lingered and a thin layer of sand lined the floor. They arrived early afternoon and dumped their bags in their rooms. They changed quickly and headed down to the beach, past an endless parade of chip shops, cafés, tattoo parlours and nail salons, before reaching the small, fly-ridden walkway that led to the sand. They walked along the shore until they reached a secluded area, away from screaming kids and fully grown men intent on digging deep holes in the sand, for reasons best known to themselves. The group laid out their towels and the girls took off their shorts and T-shirts, revealing bright yellow and pink swimwear underneath. Though he'd seen Amy naked many times now, Will had not seen her in a bikini before. He sensed this was something she was nervous about, so he gave her a reassuring smile. Charlotte shared no such worries. She pulled out a clunky Polaroid camera from her bag and ordered them to pose for a photo. Will wrapped his arm around Amy and they grinned cheesily, waiting for the click and whirr of the camera. Charlotte sat down on her towel, her red hair tied back and skin alabaster in the sun. She shielded the freshly printed photo from the light with a cupped hand.

'Not bad, you can have that,' she said, passing it to Amy.

Amy lay on her back thumbing through a sandy paperback, squinting her eyes in the sun. Will, shirt off, on his front next to her, flicked through *Misshapes* fanzine, his heart skipping a beat as he got to the reviews section.

SharpShooter – The Outsiders

Hailing from the sleepy town of Malford, these boys take the frustration of small-town life and turn it into a beguiling noise. 'The Outsiders' recalls early Manics and Placebo, while 'No Love Lost' recalls The Stone Roses and would be at home on any of the Shine compilations. Lyrically, the familiar themes of boredom and teenage alienation are the backbone, but there's enough interesting turns of phrase to keep

things fresh. It can't be long before major labels come
knocking.

Will tried to quell the queasy feeling in his stomach, his head spinning at the words 'major labels.' He passed it to Jake, his skinny body basking in the sun. 'Fuck – that's one for the scrapbook.' He beamed.

'We are definitely drinking to that later!' said Charlotte, handing the fanzine to Amy with a grin.

After chatting giddily in the sun, they went for a swim. The water was grey and deceptively cold, churning endlessly. Amy wrapped her arms around Will and they bobbed up and down together, kissing, her hair wet and tangled and lips salty. Jake cupped his hands under the surface and flicked them upwards, splashing Charlotte; she smiled and splashed him back, a big, dirty waft of water.

Will and Amy hotfooted it across the pebbles and shells, back to their towels, leaving the other two out there, climbing all over each other. Amy's slender, wet body glistened in the sun as Will lay with his arms draped over her. She unclipped her top and tucked it under herself to avoid tan lines.

'Are you going to do my back, mister?'

Will squeezed a dollop of sun lotion onto his hand and rubbed it into her warm, sandy skin. He moved his hand to the small of her back and then along her thighs. He could take her right here, right now.

'Feels good,' she whispered.

'Just warming you up for later,' said Will, kissing her neck.

Amy smiled mischievously and turned on to her back. They lay in the beating sun together and sucked on a shared ice lolly, the juice running down through their fingers and making sticky dark puddles in the sand.

After the beach, the group headed past the rundown crazy golf course to the funfair. Boy racers – shirts off to reveal their pasty, bony bodies – held court on the gravelly tracks, looking them up and down with disdain as they passed. Garish music from a dozen different rides and machines collided in the air. The girls went off to pick up some chips and Jake pushed a 2p into the slot machine, timing it badly; it landed on top of a stagnant heap of coppers.

'I don't get these machines. You are putting in 2ps to win more 2ps?' said Will.

'Yeah?'

'Well, who wants more 2ps?'

'All right, big spender, there's a 50p one over there.' Jake chuckled, pointing at another row of machines; knock-off Made in China toys staring out from them. 'You should win Amy one of those, she'd love that.'

'No one loves that naff crap.'

'It's the gesture,' replied Jake. 'Women are hard-wired for that stuff, like a caveman returning with a kill.'

Will was dubious but slid a shiny coin in the slot and jostled the joysticks with his clammy hands. The metal claw stuttered to the right and came down hard, hitting the fluffy blue duck in the head but with no real purchase. His second and third attempts were no better.

'Let me try,' said Jake. 'You're paying, though.'

His first attempt was no better than Will's as he struggled to get to grips with the controls. On his second attempt, the claw lifted a fluffy blue fish up a few inches from the pile, before dropping it. On his third attempt, the claw came down flush and clasped itself around a cuddly black and white penguin with an orange beak, gripping it firmly, lifting it up and dropping it into the tray.

'Wheeey,' they cried in unison, high-fiving.

'Here you go mate.' Jake winked, digging it out and passing it to Will.

*

Back at base, Charlotte turned on the taps and watched the water slowly filling the small white porcelain bathtub. She lay in the soapy water for nearly half an hour, her skin red and sore from the sun as she ran a flannel over her body.

'Anyone want the water?' It's lukewarm still,' she shouted, getting out and wrapping herself in a towel.

'You know, when he was young, Luke didn't realise that lukewarm was an actual word. He thought it was just what his mum said when the water was the right temperature for him,' said Jake.

The others burst out laughing.

'That can't be true,' Will spluttered.

'I'll have it,' said Amy. 'Want to join me, Will?' she said, glancing at him.

Will had never had a bath with a girl before. In films, couples always tessellated effortlessly, but the reality was far less erotic than the fantasy; he couldn't get comfy because of the taps and was self-conscious about the way his balls floated to the surface.

That evening, they ate pesto pasta salad and drank cheap white wine on the balcony, the portable stereo drifting away gently in the background. Neither of the boys had tried pesto before; it's flavour nutty and distinct as they washed it down with the wine. They chatted about the upcoming elections and exam results day, which was looming large. What was going to happen in September, if Amy and Charlotte got into university, was the elephant in the room – none of them wanting to be the one to ruin the moment.

After a dessert of strawberries and cream, Jake and Charlotte disappeared off to the bathroom and came back moments later, giggling. Jake wiped his nose with his sleeve, and Will pretended not to notice the clump of white residue that lingered on it.

'Let's play Never Have I Ever,' suggested Charlotte.

'What's that?' asked Will.

'It's a drinking game. You have to say something you've never done, and anyone who has done it has to drink two fingers' worth.'

'But we're drinking anyway, so why don't we all just drink at our own pace?'

Amy rolled her eyes and nodded knowingly towards Charlotte. Jake glared at Will and he quietly relented.

'OK, I'll start. Never have I ever smoked weed,' said Amy.

'What?' said the others.

'Never fancied it,' Amy shrugged. 'Plus my dad would kill me if he found any in the house.' The others all drank two fingers.

'Never have I ever been caught masturbating,' said Will.

'I think the lady doth protest too much.' Jake chuckled. Amy and Charlotte shook their heads and kept their glasses firmly in their hands. Jake downed two fingers.

'No way!' cackled Charlotte.

'Yep. Mr Walters, Year Ten Geography field trip. He just turned around and went back out again. Didn't even get into trouble for it,' he said proudly.

'OK, my turn. Never have I ever had a threesome,' said Charlotte. Will and Jake looked at each other, their drink remaining stationary in their hands, as Amy sheepishly sipped her wine.

'Amy, you dark horse!' screeched Charlotte.

Will felt a pang of jealousy land in his stomach as he tried to meet Amy's eye. She stared down into her glass.

'You've never told me about that,' he said.

'Why would I have?' Amy shrugged.

Will glared at her. 'Because you're my girlfriend, perhaps?'

Amy furrowed her brow. 'Yeah, but I wasn't then.' She took another sip of her drink, thinking about what to say next. 'I was wasted at a party. I wouldn't do it again.'

Will took a glug of wine and said nothing.

'Anyway, we're playing a game, Will, it's not like I just randomly blurted it out.'

Will sat there, staring down at his lap, face like thunder. The CD they were listening to came to an end, but no one got up to change it, and the music was replaced by a distant buzzing in his ears.

'You're sulking now, aren't you?' said Amy.

Jake and Charlotte shot each other an awkward look.

'It was before we met, I just don't see the relevance,' said Amy.

Will downed some more wine. 'I think it's relevant if my girlfriend used to be the village bike.'

Amy screeched her chair back and bolted upwards. 'Fuck you, Will. You're setting rules about what I can and can't do with my body before we even met?'

'No, it just doesn't seem very ladylike, that's all.'

'*Ladylike* – fucking hell, what century is this?'

'Look, calm down, both of you, we've all had a bit to drink,' said Jake.

'Yeah, some of us more than just drink too,' Will interjected.

Jake gestured with his palms open. 'Woah, woah, your beef is with her, not me.'

'Just piss off, the pair of you!' cried Amy, running to the bedroom and slamming the door behind her. Will went after her and tried to make amends, softly pleading with her, but Amy sat rigid on the bed, unmoved.

'I'd like you to sleep on the couch tonight, Will,' she said, eventually.

'Oh, come on, Amy,' Will whined, his eyes bleary and head pounding like a kettle drum.

'Well, you obviously won't want to touch my disgusting body anymore anyway.'

Will scoffed. 'Fine,' he snapped, slamming the door behind him.

He went back out to the living room to defiantly continue drinking with the others, only to find they were gone, loud, guttural noises coming from the bedroom. He lay down on the couch and wrapped a blanket around himself, a familiar melancholy licking at him.

The following morning, Amy awoke, head pulsing and mouth arid. She traipsed through to the kitchen and dropped an Alka-Seltzer into a glass, watching it fizz away satisfyingly. She peered in at Will, passed out on the sofa fully clothed, tip-toed across the room and poked her head into the other bedroom. Charlotte and Jake lay there, entwined together semi-naked on top of a thin white sheet, the sunlight through the blinds illuminating their weathered bodies. On the bedside table was a small plastic bag of white powder and a credit card. Amy scowled, shut the door and left.

CHAPTER 13

A stream of kids filtered into the record store, kitted out in band T-shirts, baggy sweaters and liberally applied makeup. Tony stamped their wrists and welcomed them in; 'The Outsiders' pouring out of the sound system. Jake, Will, Luke and Pete sat in the storeroom, Lucy from *Beautiful Scum* fanzine opposite them, her dictaphone whirring away.

'Where do you see SharpShooter in a year's time?' she asked, pushing her thick black-rimmed glasses back up her nose with her finger. Jake, in a shabby black leather jacket and ripped jeans, narrow-eyed and irritable, shot her down instantly.

'We can't predict the future – all I know is that these songs deserve to be heard.'

Will tried to chip in, soften the sentiments, but Jake ploughed on regardless.

'The bands in this town, they're hobby bands, and that's fine if that's what you wanna do, but we are more than that,' he slurred. Lucy nodded. 'We won't be playing crappy back-line gigs like this anymore, that's for sure.'

'Don't print that,' said Pete.

'No, do,' said Jake. ' I believe in this band, even if these guys don't.'

The others looked at each other, inwardly cringing.

Lucy looked up from her notepad. 'And tell us about your new single. I heard it on the Evening Session the other night and was blown away.'

Will went to speak, but Jake jumped in again.

'Outsiders – that's what we are in this place. Too many people live and die in this town, but we want to see the world.' Lucy chewed on the lid of her pen and listened intently. 'I don't want to be working in a factory and wake up one day to realise life has passed me by.'

Jake's ramblings were interrupted by Tony poking his head in. 'Ten minutes, yeah, boys? There's a decent crowd filling up.'

'No worries, I think we're done here,' said Jake, standing up abruptly and running his hands through his hair. He pushed the stool to the side of the room and took a swig from the flask in his inside pocket – the neat whiskey scorching his throat.

'OK, thanks, guys. Looking forward to the show – I'll get some photos,' said Lucy, pointing to the chunky camera at her feet.

'Make sure you get my good side,' said Jake, voguing. Will shot her a look of apology, which she acknowledged with a half-smile.

Jake headed to the staff toilet and the others made their way to the makeshift stage in the corner of the store. Pete lifted his bass off the stand and plugged in his lead, sending a crackle of static through his amp. Will stomped on his fuzz box, letting the opening chord ring out and dissolve into white noise. Luke clicked his sticks together three times and the sonic onslaught ensued. Jake burst through the crowd, stepping on stage to much whooping and cheering, spitting out the opening lyrics with conviction.

Tony, who'd been promised a genteel, stripped-down set, tried to guard the racks of stock as pockets of frenzied youths leapt at each other. Hearing the commotion, more kids from the square barged their way into the store, keen for a piece of the action, pushing the front row eyeball to eyeball with the band, their frantic bodies moving to the brutal rhythm. Jake climbed up on the new SharpShooter-logo bass drum, thrashing at the cymbals with the microphone, sending a rusty bucket of noise through the speakers. Pete swung the bass above his head and thrashed at it with a plectrum as Luke hammered away on the toms. Will kept his head down, ignoring Jake in his peripheral vision, stringing together intricate chord patterns. It nagged away at him that Amy and Charlotte hadn't made it along like they said they would. For Amy, the incident in Dorset had been quickly forgotten, but Will still harboured the simmering resentment of being made to apologise when he felt like he'd done nothing wrong.

Six songs in, Jake, throat hoarse and mangling the words now, hurled his tambourine into the crowd, shouted goodnight and exited the stage. As the piercing feedback rang out, the crowd clambered to the till to buy the single, Tony producing shoeboxes more of them from under the counter.

Backstage, Will held a copy in his hands for the first time – a black and white image of a derelict building on the cover with SharpShooter written above it in chunky text – and felt an immense wave of pride. Jake paced around beside him, smiling vacantly and wiping the fresh, metallic sweat from his forehead with a small grey towel.

Luke wrapped some tape around his bleeding fingers and met his wild gaze. 'Are you alright, mate?'

'Yeah, why?' Jake snapped back.

'Just seem a bit hyped, that's all.'

Jake scowled. 'Did I miss any notes?'

'No. But your timing was a bit off at times.'

'Fuck off, look at them, they loved it.'

'Maybe just lay off the drink a bit?' said Pete.

Will looked at him squarely. 'And whatever else you're taking.'

Jake stared through him for a moment. 'Until I start messing up, you don't need to worry about me.'

Will sighed; he looked at Luke and Pete, who shrugged in defeat. Jake reached into his jacket pocket and took another swig from his hip flask.

'What was that all about, boys? They've knocked half my stock on the floor,' said Tony, bursting in from the store.

'Sorry, Tone,' said Will, staring at his feet.

'Oh, come on, you sold a tonne of records, didn't you?' said Jake.

Tony stared at him with narrow eyes, lost for words.

'We got a bit carried away, soz,' said Pete, breaking the silence.

Tony exhaled. 'It's OK, no harm done,' he said, softening.

The boys looked at each other sheepishly and Will apologised again. Tony reached over to his desk and handed each of them a few printed sheets of paper stapled together.

'Anyway, here are your itineraries for next week.'

Jake scanned the pages and took another slug of whiskey, dark spirit dribbling down his chin.

'We're going on tour, boys.' He grinned.

CHAPTER 14

Will wound his way through The Posh, *The Queen Is Dead* playing away on his Walkman. The slate-grey sky hung motionless over him, as the batteries ran low and the sound began to warp and distort. The streets here were cleaner, neater than he was used to. No crude graffiti, no caked-on spots of chewing gum on the pavements, no rusty beds and broken trampolines in people's front gardens. The band were going away for the week and Amy had invited him over for dinner so they could spend some time together first. She had warned Will that her dad could be a bit of an arse and a sense of trepidation had dull-ached in his belly throughout the day. He knocked gingerly on the front door and took a step back.

Amy welcomed him in and they sat down together on the living-room couch, further away from each other than felt natural. Margaret, Amy's mother, was in the kitchen making moussaka and a rich, homely smell filled the living room. Will had never tried moussaka before, but Amy assured him that it was just a more middle-class version of lasagne and that he needn't worry.

Roger, Amy's father, came home around 6pm, wearing a white cotton shirt with visible sweat marks and a long red pinstripe tie, clutching a brown leather briefcase. He grunted indeterminately when asked how his day was. Will couldn't remember exactly what he did, but knew it was something to do with finance or insurance. From the living room, he heard Amy's mum remind him in hushed tones that they had a guest for dinner, as she handed him a beer from the fridge.

Amy helped lay the table and Will stood idly by, not knowing what to do with his hands.

'Hello, Will, pleased to meet you,' said Roger, entering the dining room. His thick chevron moustache was greying and the hair he had left on his head left unstyled.

'Hello, Mr Stevens,' Will replied, expecting a '*please, call me Roger*' that never came.

'I hope you're hungry – she always cooks too much,' he said, gesturing towards the kitchen with his head. Will smiled a crooked smile and took his place at the table. Margaret carefully distributed the salad and potatoes and sought reassurances about the moussaka, which was, in all fairness, pretty good. Will stopped himself short of asking for tomato ketchup for the potatoes, dousing them in salt and pepper instead.

'How was your day, Amy?' her mum asked.

'It was all right, just lazing in the garden really.'

Roger hastily finished his mouthful. 'Couldn't you go to the library or something, get a head start on uni?'

Amy rolled her eyes. 'I don't even know if I have a place yet, Dad.'

Will squirmed in his chair. Amy flashed him an '*I told you he could be like this*' look that he tried not to seem complicit with.

Roger abandoned the line of questioning and turned to Will. 'I hear you are in a band, Will? Any good?'

'Yeah, I guess so, but it's not really for me to say, Mr Stevens.'

'No, of course not. Well, anyway, good luck with that.'

It was clear to Will that he thought it was a fad that would come to nothing. He wasn't sure whether deep down Amy thought the same. He needed to loosen up, but the more he tried, the more uptight he felt, as though all eyes were on him with every mouthful he took. Amy, keen to make sure that he didn't say anything remotely controversial, jumped in answering questions on his behalf. For dessert, they had rhubarb and apple crumble with lashings of thick yellow custard. Will grimaced at the tartness of the rhubarb and took a sip of water.

'Did your new intern start this week?' said Margaret, taking a spoonful of crumble.

'Yes, bloody useless he is too,' replied Roger. 'Box-ticking exercise, I reckon.'

Amy put down her fork and glared at her dad. 'And why would you say that?'

Roger looked at her. 'Because he's… you know…'

'He's what?'

'You know… black,' said Roger, holding her gaze. He could sense she had the bit between her teeth now.

'So, because your company has finally employed a black person, you think it must be positive discrimination?'

'I'm just saying that I find it hard to believe he was the

best candidate for the job. He doesn't even know his way around a spreadsheet.'

'Well, maybe you can teach him?'

Roger scoffed. 'I'm a bit busy for that, love.'

'Doing what? Playing solitaire?'

'Watch your lip, Amy, it doesn't suit you,' Roger snapped, his face prickly-red and featureless.

Amy flounced back on her chair. 'I'm just meant to sit here while you're being racist, am I?'

Will stared down at his plate, hoping Amy's mum would step in and defuse the situation, but she too looked down at her food, wishing she was somewhere else.

'Racist?'

'Yes, you think he can't possibly merit the opportunity he's been given.'

'Well, I know that Graham's son went for it, but his face didn't fit, if you know what I mean.'

Amy stood up. 'You're unbelievable.'

'Oh, here we go again. This isn't your debating society, Amy. I don't want to hear any more about it.'

'Oh, piss off, will you!' she cried.

Amy had never spoken to her dad like that before. She felt a tsunami of adrenaline and fear rush through her as she bolted out the room and up the stairs.

'Get back to this table right now, young lady! Your mother hasn't finished eating.'

Will sat there for what felt like an age, saying nothing, before quietly excusing himself and going after Amy. She lay on her bed face down, sobbing. He stood over her, rubbing her back in what he hoped was a soothing motion. She turned her head sideways to speak.

'It's the same old shit all the time. I'm sick of it,' she gurgled.

'Yeah, he was out of line,' offered Will weakly.

'I didn't see you standing up for me?'

Will shrugged. 'I didn't want to get involved.'

'Yeah, that's what people like you always say.'

Will laughed, an involuntary titter which angered Amy further.

'I think it's best if you go, Will.'

'Why? What have I done?'

'Nothing… that's the point.'

'Well, I'm hardly going to start fighting with your dad the first time I meet him, am I?'

'No. But you don't have to be completely spineless either.'

Will smirked, a reflex action that was like a red rag to a bull.

'Go home, Will. I want to be alone right now,' said Amy, still sobbing.

'OK. Thank your mum for a lovely dinner.'

'Fuck off – I'm not in the mood.'

Will crept down the stairs and fumbled with the laces of his trainers in the hallway. He could hear Amy's parents arguing vehemently in the kitchen as he opened the front door and made his escape.

*

Will sat cross-legged on his bed, strumming his acoustic softly, some evocative chords he recognised but couldn't place. The evening's events were still ringing around his brain. He slid down the fret board; the melody drifted into his head – it was 'Waterloo Sunset'. He had a sudden flashback to his dad playing the record over Sunday lunch when he was young and him humming along with it, not knowing the words. He carried on, stumbling around until he found the chorus sequence, and began to sing. He blinked hard to stop himself from weeping. He circled around again, singing it louder this time.

The poignancy of the moment was shattered by the harsh chime of the telephone. He rushed to pick it up before it awoke the rest of the house.

It was Jake, loud music thumped behind him, and voices echoed in and out.

'Will, you're awake!'

'Jake. Where are you?'

'I'm at a party with Fletch and that. Come join us.'

'I can't, it's late and we've got an early start in the morning.' Will wondered why he hadn't been invited in the first place, not that it sounded like a party he'd really want to be at.

The phone rustled and music continued to bleed through in the background.

'I just wanted to say that I love you, man,' Jake slurred.

It was clear to Will that he was off his face.

'Thanks,' he replied bashfully.

'No, seriously. I know I'm full of shit sometimes, but you and I, we've always been there for each other.'

'I know,' replied Will, decidedly too sober for such a conversation.

Jake continued to ramble incomprehensibly, spewing non-sequiturs. Will could hear him chatting to others at the party, seemingly forgetting he was on the phone at all; he waited patiently for him to return before hanging up and settling down to bed.

CHAPTER 15

Will gripped the side of the bass drum and helped Luke lever it into the boot of Mick's old white work van. They squeezed the guitars in the remaining gaps, like a complex game of Tetris. Jake ran his index finger through the thick film of grime on the door panel, scrawling SharpShooter in it.

'Where we heading first?' asked Luke.

'We've been through this – Manchester, Sheffield, then London. Sometimes I think it would be easier with a drum machine, I'd only have to tell it what to do once,' Jake jibed.

'Less weight to lug around too,' said Pete, struggling with the sluggish response of an unfamiliar vehicle.

Will looked out of the window, the cats' eyes shimmered in the late-summer sunshine. The debacle with Amy and her dad the night before weighed heavily on his mind as they made their way north. He'd wanted to call her in the morning before they left, but his stubbornness wouldn't allow. He also harboured nagging doubts about whether his mum would be OK looking after Izzy without him. The others sang along carelessly to 'Some Might Say' on the radio, but he didn't feel like it. They cracked open a six-pack of beers, navigating the early rush-hour traffic to arrive at the venue for what seemed like an unnecessarily early soundcheck time of 5pm.

All the waiting around before gigs made Will anxious. They shared a joint by the fire exit as the other bands loaded their gear in. They all had noticeably bigger amps, better drum kits and more merchandise to sell, peacocking it out on a table to the side of the stage; SharpShooter's CDs and mailing-list clipboard looked pitiful beside them.

They were opening for a 'proper' band for the first time. Signed to an offshoot of Sony, Headrush had the understandable swagger of a group of guys in their early twenties who'd just been able to give up their day jobs. They were pleasant but assured as they introduced themselves, before heading off to a boozer down the road. After soundcheck – a tedious process of hitting drums one by one and playing a few bars of each instrument while the soundman tweaked levels which would be long forgotten by stage time – they sat and had a beer in the tiny backstage area. Jake pulled a small plastic bag out from his inside pocket and placed it down on the table.

'Who wants some of this?' he said, dabbing his finger in the pearly white powder and rubbing it into his gums. Luke poked his finger in and did the same. Pete gestured 'no' with an open palm. Will glared at them both but said nothing.

'I'll be fine. We're not on for an hour,' said Jake, taking some more. 'It's boring as fuck sitting here.'

The venue filled up early in anticipation of Headrush, whose single 'Deep Heat' was getting heavy radio rotation.

SharpShooter ripped through a blistering set, Jake barely speaking a word between songs so that they could squeeze in a new one, 'Scorched Earth', into their allotted thirty minutes. He swigged at a bottle of Bud, staring vacantly at the audience as he gracefully navigated the mess of multi-plug adaptors on the stage. Will floated through the set as if he was outside of his body watching himself play, catapulted along by the pulsating beat. The PA stack trembled with the vibrations, as Luke thrashed at the cymbals and Pete wove his filthy bassline in and out. Jake dropped the mic to the ground with a deafening thud and exited the stage. The others finished in a flourish of cymbals and wailing feedback, met by generous applause and a flash of disposable cameras.

Will packed away his FX pedals, folding the setlists neatly into his guitar case to be used again. It had gone well, but he couldn't help but think that the set was missing the nuances and dynamics that usually made them so compelling. Pinning the audience to the back wall with noise felt like a cheap trick.

Headrush waltzed on stage a little after 10pm, filling every inch of it. The singer, unsuccessfully rocking both a trilby and aviators, strummed an acoustic and sang by-numbers lyrics about '*shining on*' and '*catching you when you fall*'. The crowd of teenage girls lapped it up, wolf-whistling and crying out, 'I love you Jay,' between songs. The guys stood at the back next to the musos with their arms folded, sipping on cider with 'impress me' faces.

'What do you make of them?' asked Will.

Jake took a slug of beer. 'They're alright. We're much better, though.'

'You think?'

'Yeah, listen to what he's singing. It's all shite. "*Your love is like a river.*" What the fuck does that mean?'

'It's a metaphor.'

'Actually, he says it's *like* a river, so it's a simile.' Pete grinned.

'You're not helping.' Will laughed.

'I trust in you, Will. I trust in your words,' slurred Jake, putting his arm around him. 'You're my best mate, and if you believe in your words, then I do too.'

Will smiled, a smile laced with pride and responsibility.

'Well, I can't sing them like you,' he mustered.

Pete looked at them both. 'Can you two stop wanking each other off, please?'

*

Will leant his head against the windowpane and counted the pylons by the side of the motorway as they passed. They stopped at a service station and stocked up on overpriced pasties, crisps and chocolate bars, before winding through the Yorkshire Dales; the low sun rendering them a shadowy canvas. They passed around a spliff and Pete explained how his parents were adamant he should be going to university instead of deferring. Will felt like his mum was past caring – one of the benefits of the bereavement.

An hour or so later they arrived at The Leadmill. The headliners Tailspin welcomed them like long-lost brothers, letting them use their drum kit to save them lugging theirs in and setting it up. The Sheffield crowd was sparse but, digging SharpShooter's rapid-fire set, drifting closer to

109

the stage with each song. The gang felt like road-hardened veterans, transitioning seamlessly between songs, Jake's performance just on the cusp of madness – some nights they were almost as good as they thought they were.

'That was great, guys,' gushed Raz, Tailspin's bassist, dressed in baggy dark blue jeans and a zip-up Adidas track top, although he looked like he'd never seen a track in his life. 'What are you doing later? We're having an after-show if you fancy it?'

'Yeah, sure,' said Jake, without consulting the others. Will looked at him, narrowing his eyes slightly, a look he hoped conveyed his reluctance.

'What?' Jake shrugged. 'We'll check into the hostel after.'

The venue filled up swiftly for Tailspin; a small group of girls in the band's T-shirts shoved their way to the front. 'This is our new single, it's called "Instant Honey" and you can get it over there,' mumbled their singer, gesticulating towards the merch table. 'Go and see Beth and she'll sort you out with it.'

Beth looked on, beaming at her small sense of responsibility, curly blonde hair framing her face and tight green Sleater-Kinney T-shirt accentuating her figure.

The after-party was in a small ground-floor flat at the end of a narrow, poorly lit cul-de-sac. Pete reluctantly parked the van outside, throwing an old painting and decorating sheet over the gear. Inside, the apartment was thick with smoke, the crappy stereo pumped out Ocean Colour Scene and the guys sat cross-legged on the floor, sipping on a stubby each.

'Where are you guys from?' asked Beth, nestling herself down beside them.

'Malford,' they answered in almost perfect unison.

'Never heard of it.' She smiled.

'Most people haven't,' replied Pete.

'You boys want any of this?' asked a guy with lank, dark hair, cutting up some coke on the coffee table with his bank card.

'Thought you'd never ask,' said Jake, sidling up beside him. He put the rolled-up tenner to his nose and hoovered it up. Luke and Pete took their turns next, each one trying to outdo each other with their appreciation of 'the gear'. Will knew they were both full of shit.

'Your turn, Will,' said Jake.

'I'm good,' he replied.

'Will's the serious musician. Doesn't touch the stuff,' said Jake mockingly to his new friends. Will clenched his jaw together and said nothing. He didn't mind a bit of weed, but throwing harder stuff into the mix just wasn't for him.

'We've got some tabs too, if you want in on them later,' said the greasy-haired guy, and Will watched on as Jake flashed him a hungry smile.

Hours passed as they chatted about the charts ('bunch of posers') and the local music scene ('not up to much'). Tailspin recounted tales that Beth had evidently heard a thousand times before, but Jake, in particular, was enrapt. Will picked at the label of his beer with his thumbnail and drifted in and out of the conversation.

'We better head to the hostel soon,' he said, tapping Jake on the shoulder.

Jake looked at him for a moment. 'Yeah… about that… I gave them some of our cash for the gear. Only fair.'

'You did what?!' seethed Will.

'I gave them fifty quid for the gear.'

Will felt his face raging. 'Well, that's great. Where we gonna sleep now?'

'I dunno. In the van? On the floor here? Just lighten up, will you?'

'For fuck's sake. Can you ask us before you spend the band's money in future?'

'Yeah, I'll be sure to submit an application,' said Jake. The hangers-on laughed. Pete and Luke remained silent, unwilling to pick a side.

'You can be a right prick sometimes, you know that?' said Will, flouncing off into the kitchen and out the side door. He sat down on a rotting wooden bench in the garden, head in hands, mind spinning.

'You're the bassist, right?'

He looked up, startled. Beth was standing over him and offered him a menthol cigarette from the carton. He declined with his hand.

'Guitar,' he replied, running his fingers through the back of his hair. 'How do you know the Tailspin guys?'

'Went to uni with them. They're sound,' she said, taking a drag. 'They throw me a tenner and some free drinks and I get to watch the bands – could be worse. I'm pretty sure they could do their own merch, though. I'm hardly swamped.'

Will laughed; he didn't mean it to seem unkind but worried that she might take it that way.

She took another drag and lowered herself down next to him on the bench. 'You boys were all right, you know.'

'Cheers,' said Will, shivering slightly with the cold.

'Singer loves himself a bit, though,' added Beth, unintentionally blowing smoke in his face. Will noticed a slight chip in her front tooth and wondered how she'd got it.

'Getting a bit heavy in there, isn't it?' she said, accidentally brushing his arm with her breasts.

Will nodded. 'Idiot's spent our hostel money.'

'Just crash here. I don't reckon they'd even notice, to be honest.' She smiled. 'Don't expect to get any sleep before 5am, though.'

Will wasn't sure what she meant by this; was she flirting? He disliked himself for the pleasure he took from the idea that she might be. *What would Amy think? Would she even care? Were they even together anymore?* He tried to shake her from his mind and focus in again on Beth, her restless eyes kind and alluring.

'You're pretty, you know that?' he said.

'I'm aware.' She smiled.

Will stifled a genuine laugh.

'Whaddya say we bagsy the bed upstairs before anyone else does?' she said.

Will nodded and followed her up the stairs, his stomach flip-flopping with each step. They lay in the bed together, fully clothed under the covers, chatting in whispers. The room was dark, just the light from a single streetlamp coming through a gap in the curtains. Beth snuggled up against him, her chest warm against his body. She looked him in the eye and kissed him suddenly. Will kissed her back, ignoring the wave of guilt that passed through him.

'I've kind of got a girlfriend,' said Will softly.

'What happens on tour…' Beth giggled, putting her hand on his crotch. It started to harden, and he hated himself for it. He kissed her again, her lips wet and boozy. He put his hands under her T-shirt, her breasts were cold and soft as

113

he pawed at them. Beth pulled her T-shirt up over her head and continued to touch Will through his jeans, her tongue in his mouth.

'Sorry, I can't do this,' said Will, breaking away from her lips and turning away on his side. Beth exhaled and sat up sharply. She said something that Will didn't catch. He apologised again anyway. He lay there on his side, his head a cement mixer, and shut his eyes.

He awoke a few hours later, the fledgling sun drifting through the blinds and birdsong chipping away at his head. He extradited himself from Beth's arms without waking her and traipsed downstairs. Luke and Pete were crashed out on the sofa. The rest of the guys were still up, looking like approximations of themselves, hair sticking up, eyes dark and lifeless, babbling nonsensically, the strains of Portishead trickling through the air.

'Will – there you are, you want some?' said Raz.

Will shook his head. 'No, thanks. I'll go wait in the van.'

CHAPTER 16

The mood was cold and irritable as SharpShooter snaked their way down south, Jake in the front seat, sleep-deprived and struggling with the cumbersome map, while Pete cursed the London rush-hour traffic. The venue for the evening was one of the numerous Camden toilet venues that had drinkers in the front bar and live music in the back. Jake sat agitated on a bench in the corner of the room, amps and guitars around them, slivers of sweat running down his forehead.

'Riptide, please,' shouted the soundman from the stage.

'Urgh, thought we were soundchecking next.' He scowled. 'I'm heading out to get some food, coming?'

'Nah, too nervous. I'll eat afterwards,' said Will.

Pete turned to look at him. 'What you nervous for?'

'These places, they're full of A&R scouts on weeknights, we need to be shit-hot to impress.'

'Yeah, but I'm not sitting around for another half an hour,' said Jake.

'OK, be back for half past, though,' said Will.

Jake swept his fringe out of his eyes and nodded. Itching to just get on stage and sing, he threw on his jacket and headed for the exit. He stepped out onto Camden High Street, a cacophony of different songs playing from boom boxes. He headed past the garish souvenir shops, and blokes surreptitiously offering pills, towards the lock. He was on a downer; the need for a pick-me-up nagged away at him. He stopped short of the various food stalls at the entrance to the market and ducked into an old-style boozer, slipping past a clutch of punters at the bar to the toilet. He pushed his way into the cubicle and pulled out a baggie from the inside pocket of his jacket. He tried to block out the stench of piss as he racked up a line on the top of the cistern. He rolled up a ten-pound note, pressed one finger to his left nostril and snorted as hard as he could with his right. A rush of air hit him, followed by a chemically aftertaste trickling down the back of his throat. He brushed what was left of the powder back into the bag and headed back out into the pub. He ordered a pint of Guinness and sat supping at it at the bar.

A few moments later a wizened man, yellow-stained beard and green military surplus jacket, sidled up beside him, spitting as he spoke.

'You in a band?'

Jake turned, looking him up and down. 'Yeah. How'd you know?'

'Everyone is around here,' he said, sitting down on the stool next to him. 'Mug's game. I used to play with Elvis Costello and Bowie in the '70s. Never made a penny really.'

Jake nodded politely, his head feeling dense and fuzzy.

'Want my advice?'

116

Not really, thought Jake, letting him continue anyway.

'Make the most of it – it'll be over in a blink.'

Jake smiled, warming to him slightly. 'You've gotta tell me what it was like to work with Bowie.'

The stranger bought Jake another drink and regaled him with questionable tales of touring Europe with Ziggy Stardust. Jake listened with a sense of wonder, imagining what it would be like to play in a different country every night, to appear on Top of the Pops – the girls, the money, the fame. Suddenly, he caught sight of the clock behind the bar.

'Shit, I gotta go,' he said, scrabbling out of the pub and back to the venue.

Will sat there, arms folded. 'Where you been?'

'Just for a drink down the road. Got chatting to this guy who said he used to play with Bowie.'

Will baulked. 'Well, we've missed our fucking soundcheck. We've put the gear on the stage and will have to just plug and play.'

Jake shrugged. 'They're a waste of time anyway.'

The lack of apology irked Will greatly; he bit his lip and said nothing.

To the untrained eye, the show that night was fine, mistakes were minimal, but the set lacked the usual energy and conviction. The sound was muddy and Will's fingers felt leaden on the fretboard as his guilty head thumped with each kick drum. Jake stumbled around the stage with a surliness, swigging from a bottle of Jack Daniel's; his voice unusually strained and distant. They finished to muted applause from the sparse crowd, downed a couple of beers, got their fee from the promoter and left during the last band.

The gang sat in exhausted silence in the van on the way to the hostel. The rain lashed against the window, blurring the lights of passing vehicles. Pete, jaded and despondent, turned the radio on. He decided music was too much and settled for a late-night talk show instead. Jake zoned out at the words 'Foreign Policy' but suddenly remembered that he still had a tab left in his coat pocket from the night before. He reached in, pulled it out and discreetly popped it under his tongue. It fizzed slightly before disintegrating in his saliva.

'Did we sell any CDs?' asked Will.

'Two, I think,' said Pete.

'Well, that was pointless then,' huffed Luke.

Will shuffled in his seat. 'You think they'll have a phone at the hostel I can use? I need to call Amy.'

'Can't you even go three days without speaking to Yoko?' tittered Jake, turning to seek approval from the others.

'Oh, fuck off, will you, Jake?' Will snapped. 'I've had enough.' He felt his blood begin to simmer. 'I don't know what Charlotte sees in you, you treat her like crap.'

Jake blinked his eyes slowly. 'Oh, you're defending Amy's honour now, are you? You weren't thinking about her last night when you were cosied up with the merch chick.'

'Leave it out, you two, I'm not in the mood,' hissed Luke.

Will said nothing. He raked his teeth against his lip, but no words travelled from his brain to his mouth.

They checked into the hostel in frosty silence. Their room was small and damp, with rusty bunk beds, bedding with ominous stains and furry black spores cultivating on the ceiling. The wind and rain howled incessantly outside, battering the single-pane windows. They passed around a joint and deconstructed the gig, the tension between Will

118

and Jake still lingering. Luke took a drag, pushing the smoke out through gritted teeth.

'I thought London was supposed to be heaving.'

Pete took the joint from him. 'Yeah, and where were all the industry bods?'

Jake paced around the room in circles, stopping dead to speak. 'It's a good job there weren't any. We were shit tonight.'

'And who's fault is that?' said Will.

'Well, at least I try and put on a show, you guys just stare at your bloody feet.'

Will formulated a comeback in his head but abandoned it for fear of saying something he'd regret. He picked at his teeth with his thumbnail and tried to block out the buzzing in his ears.

'Let's all just get some sleep, shall we? It's been a busy few days,' he said eventually.

'Fucking hell, he's three days into a tour and he already wants an early night.'

'I'll have a beer with you here, but I'm not going out,' replied Will defensively.

'You joking? Fletch gave me the address of a guy he knows in Kentish Town, said he can sort us out.'

'I think you've had enough, mate,' said Pete.

Jake smirked. 'I'm fine. I can be there and back in twenty. You coming?'

'I'm alright,' said Will, flatly.

'Luke, Pete?'

They looked at each other and shook their heads. 'It's pissing it down,' said Luke.

*

119

Jake struggled for a minute or so with his shoes, forcing them on still laced with his thumb. He traipsed down the grotty staircase, the tab was beginning to take effect now, the steps swirled dizzily in front of him as he gripped tightly to the banister. He exited the hostel out onto the pavement, pulling his jacket up over his head to shield himself from the driving rain. He craned his neck and peered down the road, a kaleidoscope of lights from shops and bars spiralling in his eyes; he squinted to block them out, the colours merging and distorting. He gripped the piece of paper with the address on in his hand, the inky characters moving on the page as he tried to make sense of them.

*

Luke cracked open a can of beer, made himself comfy on his bed and took a glug.

'Should we go after him?' asked Pete.

'No,' said Will. 'He's a big boy. Anyway, he's doing my head in. He'll be back in a minute when he realises he doesn't have a clue where he's going. Let's just enjoy the peace for a moment.'

Luke half-smiled and stubbed the dying embers of his cigarette out in the ashtray.

*

Jake's legs felt rubbery and his arms like tentacles as he weaved through late-night revellers. Thoughts about Charlotte, her fiery red hair and what he'd do to her when he got home collided with euphoric thoughts about

SharpShooter. He couldn't wait to start singing on bigger stages, rocking festivals and to start work on the debut album.

He headed up towards the junction, looking to his right. *Camden Station is that way, so Kentish Town must be that way*, his cloudy brain reasoned. He inhaled sharply and stepped out into the road.

A thunderous smack. Black. The hideous scraping of gravel and flesh. Jagged shards of glass. A mangled twist of metal and flesh. Blood. He lay motionless on the ground, limbs at impossible angles. He tried to breathe, but his lungs had nothing to give. A passer-by cradled his face, asking him to stay with him. Sirens echoed in the distance, dissolving to nothing. His eyes flickered. His mother's face emerged from nowhere, cooking in the kitchen – young, tall and pretty. He shut his eyes. Black again.

CHAPTER 17

Will sprinted through A&E, the others close behind him. Wounded people were being hastily wheeled around on trolleys. An angry man thumped a vending machine; a hundred anxious conversations bled into one.

He pushed through a door to his left. 'Where is he?' he cried.

An Asian man in a surgical mask and gown blocked the door.

'You can't come in here.'

'I need to see him,' wailed Will.

'Come with me, please,' said the man, shepherding them all into a small room further down the corridor.

Will's breathing was rapid and acute, his head pounding and face pale with regret.

'Is he gonna be OK?' he asked.

The man shook his head – tiny movements, left and right.

'Take a seat,' he said calmly, gesturing for the three of them to sit down.

'Tell us, please,' said Luke, hopelessly.

'I'm afraid he didn't make it.'

He paused for a beat that felt like a lifetime.

'We tried everything we could. I'm so sorry.'

Luke slumped instantly, head in hands. Pete sat rigid, stunned. Will felt a burning sensation hit him square in the throat like a juggernaut. He ran to the sink and vomited, thick yellow chunks of bile, followed by a violent convulsion of dry heaves, as if his insides were trying to exit his body. Pete followed him over, feeling like he was sleepwalking; he flung his arms around Will and they sobbed uncontrollably.

'I can take you to see him, if you're sure, but you must put these on,' said the surgeon, handing them protective masks and gowns. The trio nodded and followed him solemnly and silently down the corridor, the smell of TCP heavy in the air.

Will braced himself as the surgeon opened the door. He looked down at Jake's body, battered and lifeless. A splatter of dark red blood on the bedsheets. He took hold of his hand, icy cold and black with bruising, a tangle of wires taped to it.

'I'm sorry, mate,' he bawled. 'I'm so sorry.'

CHAPTER 18

Will lay on his bed in the foetal position, silently crying into the sleeve of his jumper, the fraying blue wool blotted with tears. A crack of light forced its way through a gap in the curtains, hurting his eyes. His mum entered tentatively, opening them up fully and handing him a small glass of water. He sat up and sipped it in slow motion, the cold water mixing with the acidic bile in his throat. In the three days since Jake had died, he'd barely been out of his room and a dank smell permeated through it. Helen ran her hands through the back of his hair and tried to sit him upright.

'Will, love, you need to go into college and get your results. They won't let me pick them up for you.'

Will dabbed his eyes with his finger.

'Are you sure you're OK to go by yourself?'

Will nodded and dragged himself to the shower, wallowing in the water, imagining the jets passing through him, as if he wasn't there. A sickening guilt lay like an anvil in his stomach. *I'm to blame for this.* He knew Jake was wasted; they should have gone after him. It splintered his heart that when Jake exited this world, they weren't really getting on. They'd never really fallen out before. There had been times when Jake had exhausted his patience for sure, but he'd always looked out for him too, allowing him to ride on the coattails of his popularity, especially at school. Will, on the other hand, had kept Jake grounded, encouraged him to read, explore music and art, and stay out of trouble. They needed each other more than they knew.

Amy had called several times over the last few days, but Will had not answered. His minor infidelity on tour felt like a mere footnote in the clusterfuck of his life now, but it ate away at him all the same.

Will put on yesterday's clothes and slumped down the hill towards the sixth form. He stopped at the tiny newsagents on the corner and pulled the *NME* down from the shelf. Elastica were on the cover, looking chic with their heavy fringes, Doc Martens and leather jackets. He flicked through it until he got to the live reviews section, stopping dead in his tracks.

Headrush, The Shakes & SharpShooter –
The Boardwalk, Manchester

First on in this midweek triple bill were SharpShooter. Filling the stage with a confidence and sound that belies their tender years, they played a short and sweet set, packed full of tunes. Singer Jake Summers swaggered around like a born frontman, channelling the jerky energy of Ian Curtis and the voice of Jeff Buckley. The future looks very bright indeed for these boys.

The last sentence cut him like a cruel joke. It was over before it had even begun. He shoved the magazine back on the shelf, turned around and left. He made his way through the steel college gates. The courtyard was eerily quiet as he headed to the gymnasium. Rows of tables were laid out in alphabetical order, a bored-looking staff member manning each one. He found his table and a kindly lady passed him an envelope. He tore the strip off it cautiously, unfolded the paper and scanned it with his weary eyes. Two Cs and a D.

Shit. *What will I do now?*

He wondered around town in a daze, saccharine music emanated from shops as he passed, irritating him. He scraped together the coins in his pockets to buy a paper cup of tea from a kiosk, lacing it with several sugars before mustering the strength to head to Tony's.

The shop was empty and Fuzzy Logic played loudly to no one.

'Will, come in,' said Tony softly, head bowed.

'I guess you heard about Jake?' asked Will quietly.

'I did. I'm so sorry. I called, but your mum said you were asleep.'

Will fidgeted with his sleeve, staring at his dirty shoes.

'We let you down.'

Tony fiddled with a dial behind the counter, turning down the music.

'Will – look at me. No, you didn't. It's not your fault, son.'

126

Will looked up at him, feeling like he might burst.

'I've got to go, sorry,' he said, fleeing the shop.

*

That evening, Will stood in the kitchen in his dressing gown, slowly buttering some toast for his dinner. Helen sidled up next to him.

'Are you OK, Will?'

He looked at her briefly before returning his eyes to the toast. 'Not really,' he mumbled.

'Look, I know I haven't been the best recently.' Her voice caught in the air. 'But that's going to stop. I'm going to be there for you.'

Will nodded, said nothing. She took his hand.

'I'm going to be a better mother to you and Izzy, I promise,' she started to sob.

Will watched the thick black mascara run down her cheek. Wrapping his gangly arms around her, he let go of the tears he'd been holding on to. Helen gently stroked his back and stayed there for as long as he needed.

Later that evening, Pete called by the house to see if Will was all right. The conversation was stilted; Pete's voice quiet and strained, Will's quivering with tired emotion, as they traded stunted memories of Jake.

As the clock approached midnight, Will tried to settle down to sleep. He was shattered but knew that it would not come easily. He put 'The Outsiders' on and listened to it loudly on his headphones, paying extra attention to Jake's voice – full and warm – and wondered if things would ever really be the same again.

CHAPTER 19

Amy's feet pounded the pavement in time to the surging music in her ears. She ran down a quiet side street and into the park, scattering a flock of pigeons as she did so, circling it several times. Seeing the same faces sitting on the benches each time, she gave them little nicknames in her head – fake tan, yuppie, wino. On the way home, she stopped outside Charlotte's. She ambled, out of puff, up the drive, past the coiffured hedges, perfectly manicured lawns and her father's shiny silver Bentley. She knocked gently on the door. A moment later, Charlotte answered in a thick towelling dressing gown, her hair converging in matted clumps.

'How did you get on?' Amy asked.

'It doesn't matter anymore,' Charlotte sighed. 'You?'

'Three As and a B,' said Amy, conscious not to smile.

'You off to King's?'

'I guess so. What you gonna do?'

'I don't know. I don't feel like doing anything right now, to be honest,' said Charlotte, tears beginning to fall.

Amy looked at her – fragile and ashen – and searched for something to say. 'I know it feels like the world is ending right now. But it will get better, I promise,' she consoled, just about holding it together herself.

'I just miss him,' said Charlotte, falling forward into Amy's arms.

Amy hugged her tightly, feeling her shiver in her embrace, rocking gently back and forth as she sobbed on her shoulder.

'One day, we are both going to be far from this place,' said Amy, stroking her hair.

Charlotte rubbed her bloodshot eyes, snivelling, she met Amy's gaze.

'Promise?'

'Promise,' replied Amy, kissing her forehead.

*

Back home, Amy enjoyed a piece of celebratory chocolate cake her mother had picked up from Marks & Spencer, the icing smudged as she sank her fork in.

'There's some champagne in the cellar, but we'll wait until your father gets home,' said Margaret.

'There's really no need for a fuss,' said Amy bashfully.

'Nonsense, my little girl, off to university.'

Amy smiled reluctantly. She flicked through the newspaper, stopping to read an article about Cambodia, and took a shallow sip of her tea.

Sometime later, Roger returned home. Amy could hear him huffing in the hallway and slamming doors.

'How'd you get on?' he said, entering the room.

'Three As and a B.'

'Well done,' said Roger begrudgingly. 'What was the B for?'

'Sociology.'

Roger tutted. 'That would have been a good one to have.'

Amy's mum shot her a sympathetic glance but offered no words.

'Have you started looking at accommodation?' said Roger, unable to resist his love of logistics.

'Give me a chance, Dad, I only got accepted today.'

'If you want to get the best halls, then I'd start sooner rather than later.'

Amy sighed; it was clear that he was in one of *those* moods.

'Who fancies a glass of bubbles?' said Margaret.

'It's OK, Mum, I've gone off the idea,' said Amy, flouncing off to her room.

*

That evening, after a terse dinner, Amy decided to call around to see Will. She'd not seen him for over a week now. She understood that he needed space – his best friend had died – but she also felt in a state of flux, waiting to return again to the life she once had. When they spoke on the phone, he was icy and curt. He was hurting, she knew that, but so was she. They had planned to keep things going long-distance while she was away at uni, but right now she didn't feel at all sure what was happening.

Amy knocked cautiously on the door. Helen answered.

'Amy, how are you?' she asked wearily.

'I'm OK, thanks,' replied Amy.

'I'm sure you heard about Jake?'

Amy nodded. *Of course I've heard about Jake.*

'Shame. He was such a nice boy. Him and Will were thick as thieves together.'

'Is Will in?' Amy asked, knowing he almost certainly was.

'Not sure, let me see,' replied Helen apprehensively.

Amy stood there anxiously as Helen pushed the door to and headed upstairs. She could hear murmuring. She strained to listen in but couldn't make out the hollow sounds. Moments later, Helen came back to the door.

'He didn't answer when I knocked on his door, must be asleep, sorry,' she said, rubbing the back of her neck. It was clear to Amy that she didn't enjoy being asked to lie.

'I won't be long, if he needs rest?'

'I'm sorry, Amy. Another time, yeah?' she said, slowly closing the door.

Amy felt a punch in her gut; she stood there frozen. *Maybe this isn't worth the effort anymore.*

CHAPTER 20

Helen rinsed out her mug with warm soapy water and placed it on the draining board. The urge to drink something stronger itched away at her, but she had made Will a promise. If he did emerge from his room these days, it was only for food or a glass of water, which he would take back with him without uttering so much as a word. She could hear the strains of the saddest music coming from his room. She would knock and ask if he needed anything but get only monosyllabic grunts in reply. From the glimpses she caught of him, his eyes were big pools of black, with bags of sorrow underneath.

She made Izzy a peanut butter and banana sandwich, her favourite, and they sat down to watch an Attenborough documentary together. They smiled at each other as the mother orangutan groomed her young, so maternal and humanlike.

A few moments later, the doorbell rang. It was Mick, Jake's father. He stood static on the doorstep, barrel-chested, with short, greying hair, his face weathered and cracked. Helen looked at him with sympathetic eyes. 'How are you coping?' she asked, although it was clear that she was looking at a broken man.

Mick looked down at his boots, worn at the toes. 'It's not really sunk in yet, to be honest,' he said, looking up and meeting her eye. 'I keep waiting for him to come home.'

Helen searched her head for something to say, but nothing seemed appropriate.

Mick, sensing this, continued. 'I'm keeping myself busy, you know, to try and take my mind off things. Been sorting through his stuff – got a couple of bits for Will actually.'

'I think he's still asleep at the moment, but thank you. I will pass them on.'

'Thanks.' Mick nodded and lifted up a tattered carrier bag but didn't hand it over.

'Sorry, I'm being rude,' said Helen. 'Would you like to come in for a cuppa?'

'Please.'

Helen didn't need another tea, all she seemed to do at the moment was drink bloody tea, but thought it would be weird if it was only Mick drinking, so she took out two mugs and stood over the kettle. It seemed to take an age to boil.

'Izzy, darling, would you take your colouring upstairs for a moment, please?'

Izzy put up no objection. She'd been told that something bad had happened to Jake, and that she might need to be kind and patient with Will for a while, and sensed that now was not the time to protest.

'It's just some post for the band and Jake's microphone,' said Mick, lowering himself down onto the sofa and placing the carrier bag on the coffee table. 'I thought Will might be able to make use of it.'

'Thanks,' said Helen, patting the bag with her hand.

'There's also a notebook. I didn't really look at it, it was too painful, but I think it's full of lyrics. Jake was always scribbling in the thing.'

Helen looked at him; she couldn't imagine how she would feel if she lost Will as well and thought it was miraculous that he even had the strength to leave the house.

'Have you started thinking about the funeral?' she asked gently.

'A little bit. Might not be for a while yet, though. There's an investigation into what happened, and they are waiting on toxicology results. The indications are that the traffic lights were in the driver's favour, though.'

Helen took a sip of her tea and listened intently.

'I just feel like I failed him. I'd heard he was dabbling in stuff, but I didn't realise how bad it'd got.'

A silence hovered between them. Helen put her cup down and tried to find the right words.

'It's not your fault, Mick. You were the one who was there for him. Will always told me how fondly he spoke of you, and how much he enjoyed working on the site.'

Mick allowed himself a flicker of a smile at the thought.

'How's Will taking it?'

'Not well. I'm worried about him, to be honest.'

'Give him time,' said Mick, taking a cursory mouthful of his drink. 'He's got good friends around him. Luke and Pete, they're good kids… And he's got you.'

Helen thought about the four of them on stage together, the colossal sound they made – bigger than the sum of its parts – and a crushing wave of realisation hit her. She shook it away; she had to stay strong right now.

'Let me know if I can help with anything,' she said softly.

Mick took a handkerchief from his pocket, blew his nose, folded it and put it back.

'Or if you just need someone to talk to,' Helen continued.

'Thank you. I've got one of those new mobile phones for work. Here's the number,' he said, handing over a flimsy off-white business card.

Helen felt compelled to hug him. She opened her arms and reached them out and he nestled into them. He felt rugged and brutish in her arms, the antithesis of Will's father.

'I needed that,' he said quietly, before turning and walking down the driveway. If he stayed any longer he knew he would fall apart.

CHAPTER 21

Will lay prone on the couch, flicking through the channels, a bowl of half-eaten Shreddies on the floor below him. He'd been awoken early by the sound of foxes fighting, or mating; either way, it was the most hideous sound he'd ever heard.

In the days that had passed since Jake's death, he had spoken to Amy a couple of times on the phone, but not seen her. She'd wanted to come over, but he wasn't ready. Some days he would sit in the garden for hours on end, letting the sun wash over his face, as if it could cleanse him of everything that had happened. He would lay back and could physically feel the summer ebbing away and passing him by. At night he would lie in bed, a ball of grief, wondering, *Why Jake? Why not me?* If he slept long enough, he would dream that he was with Jake, or his father; he'd then wake up and realise with gutting sadness that it wasn't real – his day could never recover from that. He thought about the time he and

Jake had biked out to the creek together and messed around on the rope swing there; what he'd give to do that today.

Helen stood at the hallway mirror, putting her earrings in. 'I'm off to work, love. There's some post for you on the table. Jake's dad dropped it off,' she shouted through. 'I've also left something for you. I think you should see someone. It might help.' She had been patient and kind to him over the last couple of weeks but was anxious that he needed to get back up and running again soon.

Will grunted and flicked through the channels some more. He watched a bit of a kids' show about a badger that was seemingly addicted to mashed potato, and then switched it off. He went through to the dining room table and glanced at the leaflet his mum had left for him – NHS Grief Counselling. He slid it across the table with his fingers and picked up the thick white envelope next to it. He tore it open and pulled out a printed white sheet with a crisp blue letterhead.

Dear SharpShooter,

Thank you for submitting your demo to Rock the City '97. We thought that it possessed a lot of potential and are pleased to offer you a place at our event in November.

In its tenth year, the Rock the City gathers the biggest names in the industry in London for three days of live shows, seminars, Q&As and more. Please see the attached pack for more details.

Will smiled ruefully; a week ago they would have killed for that kind of exposure, but the offer seemed almost mocking now. He leafed through the pack, stuffed it back in its envelope, took it upstairs and chucked it on his desk. He opened Jake's notebook: burnt orange cover, plastered in stickers and slogans.

We are just silhouettes, always passing, never stopping. As my worn-out soul comes to call, I wonder, do you still think of me at all?

It was too private, too raw; he closed it again. He picked up his acoustic guitar and strummed it lethargically for a few minutes. He then took a shower, hoping it would kill at least half an hour. After drying himself, he put on a baggy T-shirt and staggered across his room looking for some clean pants, the combination of shirt and no underwear making him feel like a toddler on the beach.

The doorbell rang.

He ignored it at first, but when it sounded for a second and third time, he could no longer do so. He haphazardly finished dressing and headed downstairs. It was Luke. Deep, dark circles under his eyes and a peculiar yellowish complexion to his face.

'How are you, mate?' he asked.

Will shuffled on the spot, his feet sockless on the doormat. 'Well, you know. Been better.'

Luke let out a resigned half-smile from the side of his mouth. 'I miss the daft prick, you know?'

Will nodded slowly. 'Me too.'

Luke looked at Will, his eyes swollen and lifeless. 'What about music? You been playing?' he asked.

'No, not really.'

'I was speaking to Pete and he wondered if you wanted to have a jam sometime? You know, when you're ready.'

Will furrowed his brow and narrowed his eyes. 'Jesus Christ, we've not even had a funeral yet and you want to rehearse?' His voice sounded thin and whiny. 'What even is there to rehearse for anymore?'

Luke shrugged. 'I meant just for fun.'

'Well, I don't feel much like having fun right now, to be honest.'

'You can't stay in here every day, mate,' Luke huffed.

Will felt an anger rise inside him. *Why is everyone just carrying on as normal?*

'I better go, Luke,' he said, shutting the door on him.

*

Will dabbed some Marmite on a piece of toast and hacked out a chunk of cheddar cheese with a blunt kitchen knife. Helen had tried in vain to get him to start eating again properly. After his 'dinner' he sat on the couch watching *Tomorrow's World*; they were showcasing a robot vacuum cleaner that seemed unlikely to catch on.

The phone buzzed; Helen answered at the third ring.

'It's for you, Will. It's Amy, and I'm not telling her to go away this time,' she said with her hand clasped over the receiver. Will took a deep breath and pulled himself up from the couch.

'Hey,' he said flatly.

'Hey. How are you?'

'I'm OK.'

'How are you sleeping?'

139

'Not too well. But I've been given some stuff to take,' he muttered.

Amy inhaled. 'It's not your fault, you know.'

Will said nothing; he wound the phone cable around his finger, watching it go pink from the pressure.

Amy continued, 'When Jake was in that kind of mood there was nothing anyone could say to him to stop him doing what he wanted.'

'I know,' said Will softly. 'How's Charlotte?'

'A bit of a mess, to be honest. Keeps calling me in the middle of the night.'

Will thought he should say something about Jake loving her, but he couldn't bring himself to say something he knew wasn't true.

'Can I see you?' asked Amy abruptly.

'Yeah. Soon.'

'You don't sound too thrilled.'

Will let the silence hang. 'I'm just a bit of a mess at the moment.'

Amy's voice surged. 'Look. You've lost Jake, but why are you shutting me out too?'

'I'm not. I just need time. Honestly, you don't want to see me like this.'

Amy gathered her thoughts. 'Do you miss me at all?'

'Of course.'

'Well, it doesn't seem like it.' Tears began to form, until her eyes could no longer contain them; she wiped one away with her index finger, but another one swiftly followed.

'Amy, don't be like that,' Will pleaded.

'Just let me know when you want to see me, yeah,' she said, putting the phone down.

Fuck.

Will lay face down on the bed. Everything just seemed too much right now.

CHAPTER 22

Helen ran her fingers through the back of Will's hair, trying to stick down a piece that had a mind of its own. Will wrestled with his tie in the mirror, his fingertips numb and breathing listless. It was the morning of Jake's funeral and the weather lay heavy and humid. He'd been in two minds about going, he wasn't sure if he could face everyone yet, but felt that he owed Jake that much at least.

Helen stoically accompanied him into the church. His old black school shoes clip-clapped on the varnished wooden floor. Luke and Pete were both there already, wearing what looked like hand-me-down suits, faded and too big for them. They hugged clumsily and talked of how they were all doing, but with very little candour.

Moments before the service began, Amy walked in, wearing a black, figure-hugging dress, propping up a clearly distraught Charlotte. Her hair was in some sort of complicated up-do and Will found himself gawping. His reflex was one of minor panic; he didn't know she was coming and he wasn't ready to see her. The immediate panic was followed by a twinge of resentment – she only knew Jake through him, so why did she want to be here? Beyond all this, though, she looked resplendent, celestial almost, something Will couldn't ignore, as hard as he tried. This was not the place for such thoughts, but that smile he hadn't seen in weeks, those divine eyes, those snow-white cheeks, made it difficult to banish them.

'How are you?' she asked, embracing him gently.

'I'm OK, thanks.'

She looked at him and said nothing, trying to convey '*but how are you really?*' with her eyes. Will ignored her intentions.

People took to their seats. Will sat on the hard wooden pew with Amy by his side. The mid-morning sun shone through the stained-glass windows, making kaleidoscopes of colour on the floor. He chanced tiny glances at her, trying to block his drunken indiscretion on tour out of his mind. The organ started up and Mick and his brothers carried Jake's coffin in. His Year Eleven school photo stared out from the pulpit, his hair short and gelled, his smile cheesy and forced. Will had turned down the chance to see his body in the morgue and seeing his face again, even in a photograph, choked him. Amy put her hands on his, tender and warm. Will looked down at his fingernails, thin slivers of dirt under each one, and silently scolded himself – his best friend's funeral and he didn't even have clean fingernails. The forced joviality of 'All Things Bright and Beautiful' left him cold. *Jake would never have chosen that.* He stared down at his feet and wished the whole thing would end.

Mick stumbled through a reading, something about friendship from *Winnie-the-Pooh*. He wept as he spoke and whispered, 'I miss you, son,' as they lowered the coffin down to the sound of 'I Wish You Were Here'. He had asked Will if they wanted one of their songs used, but he'd decided that even Jake wasn't quite that self-indulgent.

*

The wake was held back on the estate. The house was dusty from an abandoned DIY project and maudlin music trundled away. People helped themselves to wafer-thin ham sandwiches and an assortment of biscuits from the table. Will couldn't stomach anything. He stood solemnly in the corner with Amy, a stony silence between them.

'Do you want me here?' she asked.

'Of course,' Will replied instantly, but in truth, he wasn't sure how he felt about anything right now.

'Well, it doesn't seem like it. You've not introduced me to one person.'

'I'm sorry if you're not having a good time, Amy, but it is a wake, you know, not a networking event.'

Amy sighed. 'I know that, but you just don't seem very happy.'

'I'm not happy, because my best friend has just died,' he snapped.

'Maybe I shouldn't have come.'

Will stared down at his feet. 'Maybe,' he said spitefully.

'I came because I wanted to be here for you and Charlotte, not for Jake,' said Amy, feeling her eyes fill with tears. 'But I'm going to go now.'

Will knew that he should stop her, but it required an energy he didn't possess. Amy looked at him, kissed him on the cheek, turned and left. Will went to go after her, but as he did, Mick came over. His skin was taut and hands like sandpaper as he shook his.

'Are you all right for a drink, Will? There's some little Belgian beers in the fridge if you want one?'

'I'm OK, thanks.'

Mick wiped his hand across his brow, sliding away a trail of sweat. 'Have you boys thought about what you are going to do with the band? He'd want you to continue, you know.'

Will ran his hands though his hair, lank and greasy; the idea of playing music just seemed so futile right now. 'I dunno. It just wouldn't feel the same with a different singer.'

'Think on it, son. You boys had something special.'

'*Had* something special – that's just it, though, isn't it?' Will shrugged. 'It's all gone now.'

Mick looked at him for moment. 'Just don't ever stop writing, Will. Promise me that much.'

Will nodded. The words reverberated around his head as Mick turned to attend to some elderly relatives, filling their mugs with tepid PG Tips. Helen was stood across the room chatting to some other mums, a glass of white wine in her hand. Will glared at her.

'It's one glass, Will. I've got it under control, I promise,' she said.

Behind her, Pete, Luke and Tony clinked their beers together.

What the fuck is there to celebrate? he thought to himself.

*

That evening, as Will lay on his bed flicking through an old Q magazine, there was a knock on the door. It was Izzy. He said nothing for once, allowing her to enter.

'How was your day?' she asked.

'One of the worst days of my life,' replied Will. He wasn't actually being melodramatic, but labelling it as such made it seem so.

'OK, well, if you need anything…'

The words were too adult, he knew that his mum had put her up to it, but he appreciated the effort nonetheless. Izzy pulled a cassette from the pocket of her pinafore dress. 'Here, I made you this.' Will took it in his hand, the casing decorated in silver and gold pen, 'Songs for Will' written in her best handwriting.

'Thank you.'

'It might be a bit girly for you. But I hope that it can make you smile again.'

And, for a moment at least, it did.

CHAPTER 23

Amy stepped off the train, her rucksack weighing heavy on her shoulders. The late-summer sun left damp circles under her arms. She put her bag down on the dusty pavement and traced her finger across the cracked Perspex of the bus timetable, relieved to see that there was one coming in a few minutes. She was on her way to a campsite in South Wales for a few days, for what should have been her and Will's first holiday together. She'd not seen him in weeks. He had told her that he wasn't feeling up to going away, and neither was Charlotte, her second choice.

Will was always talking about going places, she thought – New York, Berlin, Amsterdam – all the places he'd heard about in songs. But *she* was the one doing it, and *she* was the one off to London next month too. She understood that what happened to Jake was massive for them both, but she was hurting too and couldn't sit around in Malford getting sucked into his sadness any longer.

She sat down halfway up the bus, fanning herself with a pocket map, the orange and brown floral seats distinctly seventies-looking. It trundled through the country lanes, overhanging branches scraping the windows. Her father was dubious about her going away by herself, but she'd assured him that she would call them from the payphone every evening without fail. She peered out at the fields of cows and sheep, grazing lazily in the heat. When the sign for 'Sundale Campsite' came into view, she rang the bell. She grabbed her bag from the seat beside her, heaved it up on to her back and headed down the small stony pathway. Arriving at the entrance, she headed straight to the little shop, giving the kindly man 40p for an ice-cold can of Lilt, holding it to her forehead for a moment before downing it.

A lady in a green polo shirt showed her to her pitch – by the hedge amongst a cluster of tents and caravans. Amy laid out her little yellow and pink two-man tent and fumbled with the instructions. Her dad had insisted on a trial run, putting up the tent in the garden the night before, but, as always, he'd taken over and she hadn't really followed what to do. She struggled for twenty minutes or so, the synthetic material flapping around in the breeze and the bendy plastic poles refusing to stay in their holes.

'You want a hand there, love?' asked a balding man from the tent next door, a faded Leeds United tattoo on his arm and skin lobster-red from the sun. Amy smiled and politely declined, determined to do it herself. Finally, after following the step-by-step diagrams meticulously, she had something resembling a tent. She pushed the final peg in with her boot, sinking it satisfyingly into the earth. Dusk was beginning to bite, so she lay down on top of her sleeping bag to rest her weary eyes. The lady had told her there was a karaoke night on in the bar that evening. It would probably be terrible, but she decided she would poke her head in later, after a power nap.

She awoke an hour later and groggily scrambled around for a tin of beans and little sausages in her bag, emptying them into a small saucepan on the little red camping cooker. She sat cross-legged in front of it, gnats buzzing around her, watching the blue and orange flame flicker, a sense of accomplishment rising within her. After her modest dinner, she changed into a denim skirt and white cotton vest top and attempted to apply some red lipstick and her favourite purple eyeshadow using a pocket mirror. She'd not anticipated how difficult it was to get ready when you can't stand up. When she was satisfied that her look was as good as it was going to get, she headed to the bar.

She peered through the glass door, a man in his late fifties was murdering 'Sweet Caroline'. She tentatively pushed it open and wandered in. The bar didn't have Southern Comfort, so she ordered a large glass of white wine and took a seat in the corner. She could feel the eyes of a group of boys across the room on her. She secretly enjoyed the feeling of power but hoped that they wouldn't come over. Not yet anyway.

A gaggle of drunken hens butchered 'It's Raining Men' and an old crooner, unable to accept that his club days were behind him, laboured through 'Suspicious Minds'. Amy sipped at her vinegary wine and absent-mindedly tapped her feet to the beat. The group of lads were up next, shouting their way through 'Common People', trying to outdo each other with their Jarvis impressions. Two drinks down, Amy was feeling braver now, her cheeks pleasantly warm and fuzzy;

149

she decided she couldn't be any worse than this. She flicked through the sticky laminated book and plumped for 'Heart of Glass', hoping that she'd have time for at least another drink before it came around to her turn. Will had never heard her sing, she thought. He'd never asked her if she could.

A few songs later, her name was called and she stepped cautiously up to the stage. No applause, just expectant murmuring. The compere, greying hair and jewellery that even Mr T might have thought too much, handed her the microphone. Amy gripped it with her clammy hands and a lift-music version of Blondie started up. She ran over the first line in her head; it was higher than she'd anticipated. She looked down at some small children bopping around the dancefloor with the lack of self-awareness people of that age possess. *When do people lose that?* She glanced at the lyrics, garish blue font on a yellow background, and then over at the table of lads. She spotted one nudge the guy next to him and grin. She looked away, back at the screen, steadied herself and tried to focus on the timing.

Amy tentatively sang the first line, a little pitchy but full. She ignored a wolf whistle from one of the boys as she began to move from foot to foot, getting into it and hitting the chorus with confidence. Suddenly, the gravity of the lyrics hit her. *Will and I are over.* She meandered through the rest of the song to a smattering of applause, took a self-conscious bow and headed to the bar. She felt certain that one of the boys would follow and momentarily enjoyed the hold she had over them. Sure enough, a moment later, one of them edged up beside her.

'What's a girl like you doing here all by yourself?' asked the boy.

'Apart from murdering Blondie, you mean?' replied Amy.

The boy laughed and stepped closer. 'You were all right, to be fair.'

'Thanks.' Amy smiled.

'We were watching you in the corner earlier. My mate Gaz reckons you've been stood up?'

'Something like that.'

'Let me get you a proper drink. Two vodka martinis, please,' said the boy, making a downward motion to the bar lady with his index fingers.

He was called Stu, Amy learned. He studied history at Oxford and was away for the weekend with some 'pals'. He wore a salmon-pink Ralph Lauren shirt, with a white sweater draped over his shoulders and spoke at great length about himself, sporadically catching himself and remembering to ask her some questions too. He had dark brown hair swept into a fringe, an impressive tan for an Englishman and deep-set blue eyes which she couldn't help but gaze into.

'Come and meet my friends,' said Stuart, gesturing towards the table in the corner.

'I should be getting back,' said Amy feebly.

'Back to where? Your tent? It's barely 9.30, I won't hear of it.' Stu smiled. 'Unless that's an invitation?'

'It's most certainly not.' Amy grinned.

Amy followed him to the table and was introduced to a blur of names playing plummy drinking games.

'So why are you here by yourself?' asked Stu, once they'd both settled down at the table.

'I was meant to be coming with my boyfriend, but we broke up.'

'The guy must be an idiot,' said Stu. It was smooth and he knew it.

Inwardly, Amy couldn't help but agree. She shook Will from her mind, took a sip of her drink and smiled warmly at him.

As the night wound down and last orders were called, Stu slipped his hand into Amy's and asked if she wanted to take a walk. She knew there was probably an agenda behind it but, flush from all the alcohol, she agreed. They walked arm in arm past the shower blocks, past the static caravans and down to the small fishing lake, the waxing moon reflecting softly off it. They laid down in the long grass together and he kissed her. Tenderly at first, but then he thrust his tongue further into her mouth as he groped at her breasts with his hands. Amy let it slide. *Above the shirt only, that's as much as he's getting*, she thought to herself. Stu leveraged himself on top of her and slid his hand between her legs.

'No,' said Amy, moving his hand away. 'Not tonight.'

'Why not?'

'Because I said so,' she replied firmly. She suddenly felt very detached from the rest of the campsite. An owl hooted in the distance, as if on cue.

'Come back to my tent,' intoned Stu.

'No, I'm alright. I mean, I'm sure you're a nice guy, but I'm a wee bit drunk and think I should call it a night.'

'Kiss me again,' he demanded.

Amy hesitated for a moment. 'OK. But that's all you're getting.' She moved her head towards his; he cupped it with his hand and kissed her roughly. Then, in a swift, decisive movement, he slid his hand down under her top and squeezed her breast, pinching her nipple painfully between his thumb and first finger.

'Stop it,' said Amy, rising to her feet. 'I'm gonna go now.'

'Go on, you know you want to.'

'I don't want to. Not tonight.'

'We leave tomorrow, though.'

Amy shrugged.

'And what am I meant to do with this?' said Stu, standing and pointing at the bulge in his jeans.

'I'm sure you'll think of something,' said Amy flatly.

Stu turned and began to walk away.

'Time-wasting bitch,' he muttered under his breath.

'I heard that.'

'Good,' said Stu, turning to face her. 'The girl behind the bar was flirting with me all night, but I chose you. And now you're blue-balling me?'

Amy laughed, an incredulous laugh. 'Looks that way, doesn't it?'

She brushed some grass from her skirt. 'I'm going to my tent. And don't follow me,' she said with a courage she didn't know she had.

She walked away hurriedly, not daring to look back. She expected Stu to shout something, but he didn't. As the clutch of tents came into view, she stumbled over several guy ropes before eventually finding hers and laying her head down to sleep. It had been a long day.

She awoke fully clothed on top of the sleeping bag, the morning sun beating through the canvas, turning the tent into a furnace. She was desperate for a wee, but the shower block seemed so impossibly far away right now. She thought about the night before. *Was I too hard on Stu?* No, she was right to stand her ground – he was just another posh prick with an unearned sense of entitlement.

She had no real plans for the day, and she liked that. It was what being on holiday was all about – something her father had always failed to grasp, with his rigid itineraries and allotted 'fun times'. After washing the cigarette smoke out of her hair in the shower, she made herself a pot of instant porridge on the cooker, spread a rug out on the dewy grass and lay down on it. She loaded her Kate Bush tape into her Walkman, pulled a paperback from her rucksack and began to read. The lyrics of the song intertwined unhelpfully with the words on the page. She put the book down and just lay in the morning sun, letting the music wash over her.

After lunch, she headed down to the fishing lake. Thoughts of the night before gave her an unexpected chill. She pushed them to one side; she wasn't going to let him ruin her time here. She laid down and watched a father and son cast their lines out, more in hope than expectation, and had the minor epiphany that fishing had nothing much to do with catching fish. If Will was here, he'd insist on listening to Kula Shaker or something, way too loudly, she thought. He had taken her to see them live at Brixton Academy. As the lights came up, he was grinning from ear to ear, his hair lank and sweaty, and old acne marks visible. She didn't have the heart to tell him she hadn't enjoyed the show that much. He'd once prescribed 'You & Me Song' by The Wannadies as 'their song', but she barely even liked it. It was always *SharpShooter this*, *SharpShooter that*; she would have to nod along politely to crappy tape recordings of rehearsals, or new riffs he'd written.

Anyway, she wasn't thinking about Will, not now. She wasn't thinking about her father either, whom she realised she had forgotten to call last night. She'd do it on the way back up to the site. Things were still frosty between them. She sometimes wondered if she was what he'd had in mind when he and her mother had decided to have children. He cared about her, she knew that, but if he was proud of her, then he never said as much. Soon she would be away in London, though, no longer treading on eggshells under the same roof, no longer unwittingly poking the bear.

In the evening, she read by torchlight in the tent, rattling through chapters and getting lost in another world. The muggy weather had reached breaking point and the rain beat down on the canvas. She felt safe and content inside, though, like nothing could touch her.

The following morning, she put a shabby 50p piece into the slot next to the shower for ten minutes of hot water, raised her arms up and felt it rush over her body, the flimsy shower curtain struggling to take the strain. She washed her hair with a small bottle of shampoo her mum had packed for her, before wrapping a towel tightly around her wet torso and stepping out into her flip flops.

She was confronted by a naked man. It was the guy with the Leeds United tattoo from her first day, standing there, pot-bellied, breathing heavily.

'Sorry, love, I thought these were the men's,' he said.

'It's OK,' said Amy, looking away.

'I didn't mean to startle you,' he continued, making no attempt to cover himself up with his towel, his repugnant body blotchy from the sun.

'I'm always getting mixed up.' *He's milking it now.* 'I'll leave you be.'

'Please,' said Amy.

The man looked her up and down. Semi-hard now. 'Been coming here for years, don't usually get girls like you down this way.' She glanced back at him. *How is he still naked?* She grabbed her toiletry bag from the sink, skipped brushing her teeth and squeezed past him towards the door. He didn't make it easy for her, though, and she shuddered as his hairy shoulder brushed against hers on the way out. The feeling of his skin on hers made her nauseous. She marched back to her tent and dressed hastily. Her hair still wet, she threw her clothes into her bag and dismantled the tent. Taking it down was a lot easier than putting it up, she discovered. She had intended to stay another night but would now get the next train home. She'd have to tell her parents there had been a mix-up with the booking or something. She couldn't tell them the truth; they'd take too much delight in thinking she couldn't hack even a few days away from home.

Amy sat in the window seat of the train, her chin cradled in her hand, watching the Welsh countryside roll by. She thought about Will – her parents were probably relieved that it didn't last, but for her it still stung like hell. She thought of Charlotte; she hated seeing her friend in pain like this. She pressed play on the Walkman in her pocket and silently began to cry.

CHAPTER 24

'Two cappuccinos, please,' said a middle-aged man in sand-coloured chinos, blue gilet hugging his body.

Will took two fresh cups from the shelf above him, and while the coffee was dribbling in, put the milk under the nozzle, foaming it until it was white and fluffy. He sprinkled some chocolate powder on them with little panache and popped them on the counter. His mother had suggested that getting a job would be good for him. It would get him out of the house and meeting new people, she'd said. With college over, he would also have to start paying his way a bit now. He still didn't feel much like facing the public right now but knew that they could do with the money. Daydreaming about the records he could get with anything left over got him through his shifts. Most of the customers were rude, or in a hurry, but he enjoyed chatting to a colleague called Chloe who would brighten his day by deliberately spelling customers' names wrong on their cups.

He had recently started seeing an NHS bereavement counsellor, a man in his late forties called Simon who wore woollen sweaters and asked solemn questions about his alcohol consumption, drug use and whether he was still taking care of his appearance. He was smoking too much weed, that much he knew. Helen had found the remains of a joint in a flowerpot and told him if it happened again, he'd be out on the street. He knew it was an empty threat, but he'd have to get more creative with how he disposed of the evidence in future. He hated the endless questionnaires that Simon made him fill out but found a stranger easier to talk to than his mum or his friends – as if whatever he said didn't really matter in the same way.

The evenings were getting shorter and the 'Back to School' displays were out in Woolworths and WH Smiths – life was moving on without him. He still missed Jake like hell but slowly began to accept that he was gone and understood that he couldn't let the hurt fester and embed itself in him forever. Too often in recent weeks, he'd seen the hours that should have been absorbed by sleep, met them face on while his body tossed and turned, his mind going over and over the little fictions he told himself to make the truth easier to swallow. He'd not seen Amy in weeks, she'd given up trying to contact him. He'd met up with Luke and Pete for a drink at The Griffin, but the energy between them was strained, as if they were all just paying lip service to each other with one eye on the exit.

Most days he lay on the sofa watching television, but even the laugh at the end of *Byker Grove* seemed to be mocking him. Other days he sat in the garden with a book, staring at the page, trying to read, but the words got tangled up with thoughts of Amy – her tiny movements in her sleep, the little white birthmark on her inner thigh, her imperfect white teeth. The sickly scent of lavender from the borders were a constant reminder of simpler times, of his father making arduous trips to the kitchen and back with buckets of water to fill up the paddling pool.

The neighbour's cat, Elmo, an ageing ginger tom, sometimes hopped over the fence to see him. Will gently stroked his fluffy coat until he purred, and in return Elmo pretended to listen to him talk about Amy, Jake, and the band.

His shift at the café floundered to an end and he cycled home. His mum insisted he wore a helmet, and after what had happened to Jake he didn't feel it was right to argue. Still, he worried that he looked like a giant mushroom weaving in and out of traffic. Back in his room, he took the helmet off, tossed it on the bed and tried to fix what it had done to his hair.

That evening, he decided to call Amy. He could see things with more clarity now; pushing her away as he did was an aberration. For weeks, it felt like there was an invisible force field between him and other people. He didn't have the will to haul himself up off the carpet most days, let alone go out for drinks or dinner, but he was ready to try and bridge the gap again. Margaret answered the phone. She asked him how he was in a suitably sympathetic tone, before passing the receiver over.

'Hey,' said Amy, flatly.

'How are you?' Will asked.

'I'm good.' Her voice was distant, not quite how he'd remembered it.

'What are you doing this weekend?'

'I've got plans with Charlotte.'

'Oh, I was wondering if you wanted to do something together?'

'Sorry. She needs me right now.'

There was a prolonged beat.

'Look,' said Amy. 'What happened to Jake was tragic, I know that, but I just didn't know where I stood anymore.'

Will exhaled. 'I know. I'm sorry. I wasn't myself, but I miss you and wondered if we might be able to meet up,' he said, with a hopelessness in his voice.

'I'm sure you heard – I got into King's,' said Amy.

'Yes. That's amazing. When do you go?'

'Beginning of next month.'

Will felt a crushing sickness in his stomach. 'It's not that far away,' he said, his voice verging on desperate.

'I've been fifteen minutes away for the last few weeks and that has been too much,' replied Amy.

Will scrabbled his head for a response. He could hear Amy chewing on gum, the silences punctuated with the clack-clack of her jaw. This was the sort of thing that he found adorable when they first got together but highly irritating as time wore on.

'Well, can I see you before you go?' he asked.

Amy sighed. 'I'm not sure if that's a good idea.'

'Can I come to visit you there sometime?'

'Maybe… in time.'

Will swallowed hard. 'What happened between us, Amy?' he asked, both acutely aware and entirely unsure of the answer at the same time.

'I couldn't keep caring for you, Will, you'd stopped taking care of yourself,' she said, her voice betraying no

160

emotion. 'I'm sorry, I've moved on, and I think you should too.'

Will slammed the phone down. He lay there paralysed, his heart a wounded animal, bleeding out. He put a pillow over his face and began to cry.

*

The café was dead, 'Ocean Drive' vomited out of the speakers for the third time that day. Will tried to block it out as he wiped the tabletops with a damp white cloth, crumbs sticking to it satisfyingly as he pushed them into a little heap. Amy's words circled in his head. *You'd stopped taking care of yourself.*

'Are you OK, Will? Very quiet today,' asked Chloe, silver nose ring and green bow in her tightly cropped afro. Her mother was from Malford and her dad a Jamaican who'd settled in London in the 1960s. Although she was only a couple of years older than him, she had been bestowed the power of shift manager for the day.

'I'm fine. Just a bit tired,' Will replied.

'There's no one here. You can knock off when you've finished that if you like.'

'You sure?'

'Yeah, go home,' she said, putting her hand on his, her nails painted vibrant red. Will nodded and smiled. Chloe held his gaze for a moment.

'I read about your singer in the paper a while back. That's rough luck, I'm sorry.'

'Thank you,' said Will softly.

She began to wipe down the counter. 'What are you doing next weekend?'

'I dunno, not much.'

'A few of us are going out after work, if you fancy it?'

'I'd like that,' said Will. His reply caught himself off guard, but for once he felt like he no longer had to say no to everything.

He unchained his bike and cycled home, past the park, past his old primary school – the fabricated buildings, the sandpit, the hopscotch markings on the playground floor – everything looked so much smaller than he remembered it. He thought about Amy's words. He thought about what Mick had said at the funeral. He'd promised him that he wouldn't stop playing and writing, but besides a few self-pitying lines, he'd managed nothing. *This has to change.* He cycled faster and faster, his thighs burning at the effort. He missed Amy, he missed Jake, but he also missed making music. He rushed into the house, up the stairs to his room, picked up his guitar – an old acoustic that his dad had given him – and began to play. The old nylon strings sounded warm and sweet as he strummed away at some open chords. He got the cordless phone and called Luke and Pete to see if they were free to work on a song together.

*

Luke's house was small and had that smell that other people's houses sometimes have. They cracked open a beer and sat on the bed together. Pete plugged his bass into a tiny practice amp and Luke scooped his dusty bongos out from under the bed.

'I've got this little riff,' said Will, playing an intricate pattern of arpeggios and hammer-ons.

'Like it,' said Pete, slowly picking out the root notes on the bass.

Luke rattled the bongos with his open palms as Will began to hum a melody over the top of the jam.

Luke fetched an old tape player from his father's study and pushed the play and record buttons down together. They took it from the top a few more times, Will and Pete batting melodies back and forth – the telepathy between them still there. As it came to an end, Will slid the tape out of the machine and nestled it in his pocket.

'I'll try and write some words for this.'

'So, do you want to rehearse for real?' asked Pete.

Will thought for a moment. 'You guys know anyone who can sing?'

'Not really,' said Luke, unable to stop his hands from tapping the bongos. 'You could do it?'

'Maybe,' said Will, fiddling with the tape in his pocket.

Pete leant his bass against the side of the bed. 'You know all the songs like the back of your hand. See how it feels.'

'We've been asked to play at *Rock the City* in Islington in November, by the way. Got a letter through about it.'

'Do you fancy working towards it?' asked Luke tentatively.

'Yeah, maybe. It's full of labels and publishers and stuff. Could even help us find a new singer.'

Pete nodded. 'Let's go for it.'

Luke fetched them all another beer each and they fired up the PlayStation, the blocky footballers gliding around the pitch and bending in impossible shots.

'I just feel sad about the way it ended between Jake and I,' said Will.

'How do you mean?' asked Pete.

'Well, we were pissed off with each other when the accident happened.'

Pete laughed, a small but genuine laugh that he quickly realised was inappropriate.

'I'm sorry. It's just, you were friends for over ten years and you're focusing on the half hour you fell out.'

Will crammed his guitar back in its case, zipping it up. 'I guess.' He shrugged.

'He thought the world of you. Everyone could see that.'

'Yeah, even on stage you could see it. It was pure love,' said Luke.

Will smiled, a pensive smile that didn't line up properly and his teeth hit his upper lip.

A little before eleven, he set off home, the new tune circling around his head, feeling a tipsy-melancholy mixed with faint optimism – one shade up from utter sadness on the Dulux paint chart.

CHAPTER 25

Will glanced down at his feet, his trainers swallowing up the ground as he ran. It had just finished raining and that peculiar musty smell emanated from the warm pavement. He wasn't sure if there was a name for it but thought there definitely should be. The tape Izzy had made him whirred away in his ears – the processed beats of a pop song he didn't know propelling him along. He'd never been one to go running, but he had to get out of the house. The rolling news for the last few days had been about the death of Princess Diana: 'the people's princess'. It made him so angry, all these people grieving and eulogising someone they'd never met, when he'd lost Jake and his father.

He bolted past the chip shop, the barbers and then the church. He'd gone to Sunday school there a few times when he was little. They'd played pool with their hands in the backroom – presumably too young to be entrusted with cues – and binged on cola and crisps while the adults listened to the sermon. He dashed down towards the park, past a family playing cricket with a tennis ball. He envied them – so happy, so complete. He kept jogging, his breathing becoming shallower and a stabbing sensation radiating through his stomach. *A stitch.* He bent over double and took a glug of water from his bottle and decided he better walk home.

That evening, after eating a proper dinner at the table for the first time in a while, he got out his tape player and slid in the cassette from Luke's house. The chords and the melody still sounded promising as they floated above the hiss of the machine. He flicked through his notebook, but none of the titles and phrases spoke out to him, so he decided to start afresh. He thought about what Luke had said the other night – 'Pure love' – and began to write with abandon, pausing and playing the tape again to count out the syllables.

Fragments of youth, fragments of joy,
for every girl and every boy.
And as the curtain calls, we'll take a bow.
Nothing is forever, but forever is now.
Pure love – of that I am glad,
I'm still missing the future we once had.

Sometimes he sat down to write a song and nothing happened, hard as he tried. Other times, he felt like he was channelling something from within and everything just flowed – this was one of those occasions. He picked the best lines out of all the scribblings and copied them afresh on a new page. He propped the book open with a television remote, picked up his guitar and played the song through. It felt true. It felt special.

The following morning, he brushed his teeth and gelled his hair, sweeping it to one side in the mirror. They had a rehearsal studio booked at noon. They didn't have the heart to ask Mick if they could still use the garage, so Tony had booked them practice space just out of town. But first, he wanted to speak to Amy. She was leaving for London in a couple of days and he *needed* to see her before she left. He decided he would call around, ostensibly to give her back a bracelet she'd left at his.

He fetched his bike from the shed. It was leaning lazily against the side wall, among his dad's tools and a deflated space hopper covered in dried earth. He pressed down hard on the pedals, galloping through the town, towards The Posh, taking a short cut down 'dog-shit alley' and turning left onto Amy's road. In his pocket he had a letter he'd agonised over, explaining to Amy what an idiot he'd been to let her go. His plan was to give it to her or put it through the letterbox if she didn't answer. He skidded to a stop outside hers, gently letting his bike fall to the ground. As he approached the drive, he noticed a car parked outside: a Peugeot 306 he vaguely recognised from the estate, a miniature West Ham kit in the back window. Approaching the door, he made out two shapes moving behind the frosted door pane and two sets of footsteps ascending the stairs amid laughter. His finger hovered over the doorbell, but he couldn't bring himself to press it. He opened the letterbox, peered through and noticed a pair of bright white Reebok Classics on the doormat. Will's stomach plummeted downwards. *Whose are they?* He turned back around, hauled up his bicycle and cycled away in a dazed panic. He braked hard by a litter bin and dropped the letter in. Its gushing sentiments seemed so silly to him now.

Through clouded vision he arrived at the studio. The unit was the odd one out on an industrial estate full of bathroom suppliers and panel beaters: small, shuttered premises that had all seen better days. He sat on the kerb outside, head spinning. He'd *definitely* seen those trainers somewhere before.

Luke and Pete arrived together in the Corsa, Rage Against the Machine blaring out as they swung into the only remaining parking spot.

'You OK, mate?' Pete asked.

Will looked up at him. 'Not really. I went around to see Amy. But I think she was with someone,' he said. 'I think it might be one of the lads from the estate. You guys heard anything?'

Luke looked sheepishly at his feet. 'Don't think so.'

Will lifted himself up from the kerb and looked Luke in the eye. His face looked fresher than before, eyes less sunken and black – a reminder that all things pass.

'Tell me, please. I need to know.'

Luke stared down at the ground, hands in pockets, as if being told off by a headmaster.

'All right, she's hung out with Gavin Hadleigh a few times apparently,' he said, bracing himself.

Will's stomach finished its final descent. 'Fletch's mate Gav? Bloody hell, the guy's a prick, isn't he?'

Luke nodded.

'Is she doing it just to get back at me?'

'I dunno. If it's any consolation I think it's purely a sex thing before she goes away, nothing serious.'

Will squirmed at the thought. 'I'm not entirely sure that's helping, Luke.'

168

Luke put his arm on Will's shoulder. 'Come on, mate, let's go play some music. Forget about it.'

The walls of the practice room were covered in felt and conical sound diffusers, and the PA was much bigger and better than they were used to. They set up their gear and Will pulled a crumpled sheet of paper from his case.

'I did some lyrics for that tune we were working on.'

'Let's see,' said Pete.

Will handed them over cautiously. He hated people reading his lyrics, on the page they looked like poetry, but they weren't. Lyrics had to fit the syllables of the melody, the rise and fall of the music, and to see them displayed like this made them seem inadequate.

'"Pure Love", I like it,' said Luke, peering over Pete's shoulder as he screwed on his high hat.

Will struck up the opening riff, and Pete and Luke eased themselves into it together. He began to sing, his wobbly voice solidifying as the song went on.

'*I was proud to be the one, to walk beside you in the autumn sun,*' he lamented with his eyes clasped shut. Looking at the others felt like too much right now.

'Fuck, that was good!' said Luke, stretching his arms out above his head as the song came to an end.

'We need to record this.' Pete beamed.

'I think we should do *Rock the City* – hand out this song.' Luke beamed. Will had not seen him so enthused in a long time.

'Do you really think we should do it without Jake?' Will asked.

Pete nodded. 'His dad gave us his blessing.'

'I'm not sure my voice is strong enough.'

169

'It's fine. Let's just do this one gig. The three of us, for Jake, and then we can think about getting another singer. I'm not ready to see someone else in his place yet.'

Will looked at Luke, who smiled his approval.

CHAPTER 26

Will stood at the bar, playing with the coins in the palm of his hand, running the drinks order over and over again in his head to remember it. Work at the café that day had been easy: customers had been sporadic and he and Chloe had done the *Radio Times* crossword together to pass the time. Will was especially pleased with himself for getting 'inert' – lacking the ability and strength to move – for 5 across. The irony was not lost on him. The Griffin was bustling with weekend drinkers; a thick layer of smoke stung Will's eyes as he sipped on a frothy lager and tried to tune into the conversation. Chloe put The Fugees on the jukebox and sat down opposite him. They gossiped about the café regulars and the oddball characters of the town – the old man who dressed like a schoolboy, the guy who always wore a cowboy hat, and the lady with the pet lizard she walked on a string. She told him with visible regret about how she'd flunked her exams and was stuck working in the café for the time being but was looking to do a City & Guilds next year. Will helped himself to some peanuts from the centre of the table, discreetly licking the salt off his fingers when she wasn't looking.

'Are you seeing anyone?' asked Chloe.

Will paused for a moment. 'I don't think so.'

Chloe let out a hearty, guttural laugh. 'Either you are or you aren't?'

'Well, there was someone… but it's over now.' Will sighed, he looked down at the table for a moment and then back up again at Chloe. 'You?'

'Nah, just having fun at the moment, keeping it easy.' She grinned.

After last orders, they headed to Chameleons – the only club in town. The décor had remained untouched for decades and garish posters for loss-leading drink deals plastered the walls. The DJ blared out the Backstreet Boys, raising his arms in the air and clutching his heart ironically at the choruses. Ageing couples smooched in the dry ice and cock-sure squaddies negged groups of girls in stilettos. Looking around, the pair laughed about how they were the youngest people in there by some way.

As the night progressed, the group of café workers dwindled as Will and Chloe danced together, closer and closer, their fingertips touching just for a moment. Emerging from the club a little after 1am, they picked up some cheesy chips from the kebab shop next door. The smell of vinegar cloyed Will's nose as he held the polystyrene container open for Chloe and she picked out the chips unsullied by ketchup. They ambled home woozily, arm in arm, belting out power ballads from the club. They stopped outside Chloe's house. There was a beat before she invited him in. Will hesitated, conflicted about what to do. He felt bad about Amy but couldn't be sure why. They weren't together anymore, and she was seeing someone else, so why should he still care? *If only it was that easy.*

Inside, Chloe quietly fixed them a Malibu and Coke from her parents' drinks cabinet and they headed to her room, a small annex at the bottom of the house. They sat on the edge of the bed, sipping their drinks, the conversation brisk and drunken.

'You know my parents can't hear anything down here?' said Chloe, resting her hand on his thigh.

'Uh-huh,' mumbled Will.

'Do you think I'm pretty?' she slurred.

Chloe was pretty, of that Will was certain, but even in his inebriated state, he wasn't sure whether he *fancied* her as such. She moved a little closer, her face unnaturally close to his, her breath boozy and perfume unfamiliar.

'Of course,' he replied.

She moved even closer, shut her eyes and kissed his lips. Will kissed her back, but his reluctant tongue remained in his own mouth. Chloe broke away and took a glug of her drink. She kissed him again. She struggled to pull her top up over her head. Losing her balance, she tumbled off the bed, giggling as she eventually clambered back on.

'Real smooth.' Will laughed.

She pushed Will down on the bed, straddling him. He fumbled with her bra. Unable to work out the mechanism, she pushed his hands away and reached behind her back to undo it herself. Her hands moved down to unbutton his jeans. She rubbed him abrasively as they continued to kiss. The action felt wrong, though, and nothing stirred.

173

'What's the matter?' she whispered.

'Nothing. I've just had too much to drink.'

She continued to touch him, but nothing felt right. Her nails were long and scratchy and her breath stale from an evening of cigarettes. Will's vision grew blurry, he shut his eyes to see if that helped. She continued to kiss him clumsily. He opened his eyes again and looked at her.

'I'm sorry. I've got to go.'

'What the fuck, Will?'

'Sorry.'

Chloe wrapped the bedsheet around her chest. 'Am I really that bad?'

'No, it's not you. You're great. It's just, I dunno… sorry.' His heart was broken, and in some kind of cruel pact, his body seemed to no longer work either. He sat up sharply and started to put his clothes back on, wrestling on his jeans and sliding on his cold socks.

'Sorry. See you at work,' he said, looking at her briefly.

'Whatever,' huffed Chloe.

'I don't want things to be awkward between us.'

'Well, you should have thought about that before,' she spat, as he picked up his shoes and made his escape.

CHAPTER 27

Amy sat in the auditorium, an A4 notepad and assortment of highlighter pens laid out in front of her. It was the first lecture of term, an introduction to the curriculum and the tutors who would be delivering it. She wore her black Smashing Pumpkins T-shirt under a blue denim jacket, hoping that it might be an icebreaker with someone. A mousey-haired girl in thick-rimmed glasses made accidental eye contact with her and smiled reassuringly.

Roger and Margaret had driven her and her belongings to London the day before. They'd strolled across the campus together, taking in the impressive grey-stone buildings and decorative fountains, before heading to a nearby café for lunch. Roger had baulked at the London prices and grumbled about the sluggish service as Amy tried her best to enjoy her chicken and bacon wrap. That afternoon, she'd unpacked her books from a collapsing cardboard box, putting them alphabetically on a small wooden shelf. She hadn't brought all of them with her, just the ones that would make her look clever and interesting to the outside world. She fantasised about a boy coming back to her room and flicking through them, pulling out one he'd read, and them instantly bonding over it.

There were four of them, all girls, living together in halls, each with her own room but sharing a bathroom, kitchen and small communal living room. That evening Amy had gone to the student union bar with Kate from the room next to hers, all curly brown hair and pointy front teeth. A poster behind the bar advertised a 'Fresher's Special' of Snakebite for one pound, so they demolished two each, turning their lips and tongues scarlet. The pair mingled with the other first years throughout the night, going through the same ritual of *What's your name? Where are you from? What are you studying?* with dozens of people, but none of the names seemed to stick.

The Head of English, Dr De Souza, greeted everybody and talked about the modules they would be covering and how the credit system worked, before welcoming Professor Jeremy Walker to the stage. In his mid-forties, dressed in a light grey suit jacket with dark corduroy trousers, he looked like an action figure of a professor. His hair was swept back and greying at the temples, his tucked-in shirt revealing just a hint of middle-age spread. *He must have been handsome in his day. Still is*, Amy thought to herself, before tuning in to his address.

'I want you to know that my door is always open,' he said. 'Not literally... and please knock before you come in,' he jested. The students laughed generously. 'But seriously, I love to see students with a passion for reading and learning.

I've been doing this nearly twenty-five years and it's the one thing that keeps me going,' he said earnestly.

After the lecture, Amy went back to her room to finish sorting out her stuff. The room was smaller than the one she had at home, with old-fashioned cast-iron radiators and lifeless brown carpets. She put up some posters she'd brought with her – Kurt Cobain, Brett Anderson, Audrey Hepburn – and hoped that the pre-used splodges of blu-tac would hold them.

While unpacking, she'd found the Polaroid Charlotte took of her and Will on the beach, 'Dorset 97' written under it in thick black marker pen, their smiles cheesy and knowing. She did miss him a bit, his genuine kindness and puppy-like need to please, but her mind then turned to the time they'd gone shopping in London together and he'd been patronising about her choices in the record store, as if something was only valid if he liked it too. An argument had ensued and they'd sat in stony silence on the train home. It seemed like now was the right time to move on – new city, new start and all that – but she felt oddly conflicted about it all. University was an opportunity to redefine herself; she just wasn't quite sure what as yet.

She stood up and looked at her reflection in the mirror – slender and unusually tanned, her eyes less tired than usual. Once, when he was drunk, Will had told her she was beautiful; she'd dismissed it as the drink talking, but maybe it was true. She'd not really considered herself to be attractive at all until a couple of years ago, when boys started to take an active interest in her. Before that her confidence was largely a front, to keep up with Charlotte, one that she'd found effective but exhausting.

In the common room that evening, Kate put Garbage on the stereo and they sat around drinking Archers and lemonade from faded mugs, chatting about their home lives. Saskia, straight blonde hair and chubby rosy cheeks, was incredulous that Amy didn't have her own pony while growing up and had to use a municipal one, while Emily spoke in excruciating detail about her boyfriend back home. Amy was the only single one – the other girls all attempting to keep their relationships going long-distance, something she suspected wouldn't last too long.

A little after ten, there was a knock on the door and two second-years – George and Ollie – introduced themselves, all foppish fringes and turtle-neck sweaters. The girls invited them in. They sat down, sparked up a joint and passed it around clockwise. George took a drag and ran his hands through his hair in a decisive sweeping motion.

'We went inter-railing across Europe for the summer. How about you, Amy?'

Amy drank from her mug, cupping it with both hands. 'Um, I had a few days in South Wales.'

'Oh… sounds nice.' He grinned smugly.

'It was… mainly,' said Amy. 'Sorry. Are you patronising me?'

George held his hands up in a *fair cop* motion. 'No. I mean, I'd love to see more of the UK, but there's so much of the world to see.'

Amy looked at him with narrowed eyes. 'Look, I'm glad you got to tick off some capital cities, but it doesn't make you better than me,' she said scornfully.

The other girls zoned in on the conversation, nudging each other in the ribs.

'Christ, you're full-on.' George laughed, taking another toke.

Amy folded her arms across her chest. 'You have no idea.'

George swivelled his body away from her and started to bend Kate's ear instead. Amy looked down at her lap and picked at the hem of her skirt.

Across the room Ollie regaled Emily and Saskia with tales of Berlin warehouse parties and punchline-less anecdotes about Amsterdam coffee shops. Amy tried to wedge herself back into the conversation but couldn't. The second time the joint came around, George skipped Amy out, and she looked away, pretending she didn't want any. She sipped on her drink, tepid and saccharine, her vision deteriorating. The conversation waded on around her. Sometime later, it could have been five minutes, it could have been an hour – she had no sense of time anymore – she yawned theatrically, made her excuses and sloped off to her room.

CHAPTER 28

Will eased his Telecaster into its case and slid his lucky grey plectrum, a Dunlop 60mm, into his back pocket for safekeeping. He'd been working in the café that afternoon and cycled straight to rehearsal afterwards. He was relieved to find that Chloe had called in sick, and although it left them desperately short-staffed, it was easier than facing her just yet. At practice they'd run through all their songs twice in order, the muscle memory still there for most of them. There remained a Jake-shaped hole in the room, but Will was getting increasingly comfortable with singing and playing the guitar at the same time.

'You think we'll be ready for *Rock the City*?' asked Luke.

'Yeah, should be,' replied Will, bending down to pack up his pedals.

Pete switched the PA off with a loud pop of static. 'You fancy a beer at The Griffin?'

'Nah, I'm beat. Gonna head home,' replied Will, putting

his jacket on. He strapped his guitar case onto his back and cycled swiftly towards the town. Night was beginning to fall and the batteries in his lights had long run out. He sped up in an attempt to beat the fading light home. He scooted one-footed down the drive, along the side of the house, and stowed his bike in the shed. He slid his key in the door, turned it open, wiped his feet on the mat and haphazardly kicked his trainers off.

'Hi, Mum,' he called out.

There was a commotion from the living room, two hushed voices, stifling to a silence.

'One sec, love,' replied Helen, clearly flustered. Will ignored her and strode into the living room. She was sitting unnaturally upright on the couch, her hair dishevelled and one of the straps of her top down on her shoulder. Two half-empty wine glasses sat on the table and a pair of trousers lay crumpled on the floor, next to a brown leather belt. She swept her fingers sharply through her hair, attempting to coax it back into position.

'How was rehearsal?'

'Good,' Will replied bluntly.

'I thought you were all going for a drink together after?'

'I didn't feel like it. Where's Izzy?'

'In bed.'

Will's eyes searched the room. 'Is someone else here?'

'How'd you mean?' Helen stalled.

'I mean, is someone else in the house, Mum? What else could I possibly mean?'

Helen froze momentarily, before lifting her head to look Will in the eye. 'Yes, dear. Mick's here.'

'Jake's dad?'

'Yes, we've become friends.'

'*Friends?*' Will intoned.

Helen said nothing, just nodded.

Will felt sick; hot stones plummeted to the depths of his stomach.

'Where is he then?' he asked.

'In the dining room.'

Will looked down at his feet, taking his eyes away from hers. 'How long has this been going on?'

'A few weeks. I'm sorry, love. I should have told you,' she said, fiddling with her silver pendant necklace. 'He's lost his son, as you know. I was just comforting him at first, giving him someone to talk to…'

'And now?' Will interjected.

Helen shrugged. 'You know…'

'Urgh, that's disgusting.' Will turned and flounced off up the stairs. He slammed his bedroom door behind him, threw himself down on the bed and began to sob.

Downstairs, Mick crept sheepishly back into the living room, hairy, rugged and half undressed. He pulled his trousers back on, sat down on the sofa and rested his arm on Helen's shoulder.

'He'll come around,' he whispered.

'I don't know.'

'It's just a lot for him to take in right now.'

Helen exhaled slowly, rubbing her eyes with her thumb and first finger. 'I've not had another man in the house since his father.'

Mick lowered himself down onto the sofa next to her. 'He's a good kid. Give him time, he'll understand.'

Helen put her hand on top of his. 'I hope so.'

Will scurried back down the stairs, jacket in hand. He peered into the living room and saw the pair embracing. He shook his head in disgust and bolted out the front door.

'Will, wait, please,' called Helen.

Her words trailed off as he slammed the door. He didn't know where he was going and didn't care. He wiped his snotty nose on his shoulder and stomped away from the house. A fox, rummaging through bins, stopped and looked at him, its eyes reflecting the streetlights. Will wandered for a while, stopping in the familiar decay of the park. It was desolate, with only the sound of nearby traffic drifting by. He plonked himself down on one of the swings, rocking gently back and forth. *How could she do this to Dad?* And, *Why Mick, of all people?* He looked up at the full moon, a blurry alabaster circle, sandwiched among a cluster of stars. He found it strangely comforting that there was only one moon for everyone and that it was the same moon that Amy could be looking at, at that very moment.

He slipped back into the house around an hour later, hoping his mum would be asleep, but she was up waiting for him in the living room.

'Sit down, please, love,' she said firmly.

'Why?' Will huffed.

Helen patted a spot on the sofa next to her. 'Because I want to talk to you.'

Will stood, arms folded, resolute.

'He's a nice guy, you know, Will.'

Will rubbed his eyes. 'I don't care.'

'Look. I will always love your dad, you know that, but he's gone, and I have needs too, you know.'

Will shuddered. 'So every time I've been at practice, Mick's been around to get his end away, has he?'

183

'Don't talk like that, Will,' Helen scolded. 'It's not like that. I'm lonely, and I like having him around. He's helping me get myself together. Helping with my drinking.'

'Behind my back, though, Mum?'

'We were going to tell you in time.'

'Well, I guess I've saved you the bother now.'

Helen exhaled loudly.

'I'm going to bed,' said Will.

Helen watched him walk away for a moment. 'He really loved you, you know.'

Will turned to face her again. 'Who?'

'Your dad.'

Will scratched at the back of his neck. 'Goodnight, Mum.'

'Do you remember the time on holiday, when he drove all over town just to find a pump for your football? Or when he did your paper round in his car for you that time you were ill?'

Will's eyes rolled towards the ceiling. 'What's your point, Mum?'

'I haven't forgotten those things, and I haven't forgotten about him either. But that doesn't mean I need to spend the rest of my days alone.'

Will grunted, a noise that Helen took some encouragement from, although it was hard to fathom why. She put her arms around her son, who didn't resist, and squeezed him tightly. Will stayed there for a moment, before wriggling free.

'What about you anyway?'

Will sucked in a breath. 'How'd you mean?'

'What's happening with Amy?'

'I don't know. I think I've blown it. She's away at uni now.'

Helen looked at him sympathetically. 'Maybe you should write to her? See when she's back next.'

Will nodded, exhausted. 'We're doing that gig in London in November. I thought I'd invite her to that.'

'Good idea, that way it's on her terms. But give her space, though, if that's what she wants.'

Will felt queasy at the idea. November seemed so long to wait. He went upstairs, sat down at his desk, put some music on, ripped a page out of his notepad and began to write to Amy.

CHAPTER 29

Amy sat cross-legged on her bed, skimming through her required reading and scribbling notes in her exercise book. The light outside was waning and the radio hummed away gently. Her concentration was broken by a knock on the door. It was George.

'Amy, I hope you don't mind. I was just calling by to say sorry about the other night. I didn't mean to be a dick.'

She stared at him for a moment, floppy chestnut-brown fringe, buttoned-up light blue cotton shirt; his was a face that had surely never lacked in confidence.

'It's OK, I may have over-reacted.'

'I got you this to say sorry,' he said, handing her a bottle of Pinot Grigio.

'Thanks,' said Amy, taking the bottle from him.

'We could crack it open now, if you like?'

'It's a little early for that, isn't it?'

'We're students, we operate in a different time zone.' George smiled.

'OK, you can come in for one,' said Amy, opening up the door fully now.

She watched George survey the room with his eyes, wondering what he made of her choice of posters, the books on the shelves, the music that was playing. She swung her desk chair around and George straddled it. She turned the radio up a notch and poured them both a generous glass of wine. She sat down on the bed and they talked about King's, her icy veneer softening as he held her gaze and spoke with well-oiled charm about the history society and his friends on the rowing team. He suggested that she looked into joining the running soc. Amy smiled self-effacingly and made a mental note of it.

Later, when conversation floundered, he stepped across the room, slowly lifted her chin with his hand and kissed her.

Amy grinned, her lips still tingling.

George looked at her. 'I wanted to do that the other night.'

'So, why didn't you?' asked Amy.

'You were too busy hating me.' He laughed.

'Yeah, I'm sorry, I wasn't in the mood.'

'Mood for what?'

'The party. Meeting new people. All the bullshit that comes with it.'

'And now?'

'I've got a higher tolerance for your bullshit.' Amy laughed.

'It's OK, I'll say no more.' George smirked. He sat down on the bed next to Amy and stroked her back with the flat of his hand; she felt every sinew of herself come alive. They kissed again, longer this time. He lifted his shirt up over his head; his chest was svelte, tanned and roped with muscle.

'You aren't going to just sleep with me and then ignore me for the rest of term, are you?' said Amy, breaking away from the kiss. George shook his head dismissively and kissed her again, letting his tongue linger; he didn't have to answer her properly that way. He slipped his hands under Amy's skirt and slid her pants off. Amy slowly unbuttoned his jeans and began to give him head. She'd never done so in such vivid daylight before and felt acutely self-conscious as he looked her in the eye. George, sensing this, pulled himself away. He fumbled with a johnny for a moment, before easing himself into her. Amy gasped and clung to his rugged shoulders with her nails. She gazed up at him, letting out tiny involuntary moans as he moved in and out, quicker and quicker, deeper and deeper, before shutting his eyes, grunting and collapsing in a heap on the bed.

Amy lay there semi-clothed, staring up at the ceiling. She put her hand in his, large and warm. He held it for a moment, before letting go.

*

Will marched at double-speed across the town square, the cold drizzle bouncing off his hood. He pushed the door of Tony's open; the bell chimed as he entered.

'Ah, William. How are you?' asked Tony.

'Bearing up a bit, thanks, Tone,' Will replied, heading straight for the new releases.

'Not much out this week, I'm afraid,' Tony called across the shop.

Will continued to browse the shelf, flipping over a couple of CDs to check the track listings.

'Have you heard the new Bjork record?'

Will shook his head. Tony came out from behind the counter and passed him a thin cardboard case with her elfin face on it. 'Here, take this promo copy, I'm not really allowed to sell them anyway.'

'Thank you,' said Will, running his thumb over the smooth label.

A silence began to germinate. Will racked his brain for something to say, before Tony leapt in to save them both.

'Will, I can't imagine what you're going through, but if you ever want to talk…'

Will shot him a placid smile. 'Thanks, but the latest situation is just a bit *too* messed up to talk about.'

Tony nodded. 'I understand. But I'm always here, you know that.'

'I appreciate that,' said Will in hushed tones. He had the strange urge to hug him but decided better of it. He took a quick flick through the 99p cassettes by the till, deciding to save his money and head to Baker's Oven for a sausage roll instead.

'Let me know what you think of Bjork,' shouted Tony, as Will exited out onto the square. He passed Mothercare, British Home Stores and the hot dog stand pumping out the smell of fried onions, when he saw her up ahead. Chloe. He considered ducking into Oxfam, but it was too late: she'd seen him.

Chloe, dressed in a shabby black leather jacket, did a half-wave with her hand, stopping right in front of him.

'Hey,' mumbled Will.

She fiddled with the strap of her handbag, adjusting it slightly on her shoulder.

'Look, Will, we are bound to be on shift together again soon. We may as well have this conversation now. Get it out of the way.'

Will nodded slowly and let her continue.

'We'd both had a bit too much to drink. No hard feelings? …No hard anything with you, eh?'

Will's face flushed deep red.

'Sorry, that was mean. I know you've got a lot going on right now.'

He stuffed his hands in his pockets and stared sullenly down at his shoes, dirty with holes in the toes. 'It's OK. I'm sorry, I shouldn't have led you on. I'm just not ready for something new right now.'

'Want my advice, Will? Your ex – forget about her, concentrate on yourself for a bit.' Chloe took an audible breath. 'This world is full of boys like you, just waiting for girls to make them happy – it's a sure-fire way to be miserable.'

Will assimilated the words in his mind; they made sense, but that didn't mean he wanted to hear them.

'You need to be proud of yourself again first; the rest will follow,' she continued.

Will nodded and looked at his wristwatch overtly. 'I better go, Chloe. I'll see you around,' he said meekly.

On the walk home, he replayed what she'd said over and over again. Deep down, he knew she was right, but that didn't make it any easier to swallow.

CHAPTER 30

It was a dull, overcast autumn afternoon and Amy found herself in Professor Walker's office for the second time that day. She wasn't sure how or why, but here she was. She'd had a diarised session with him that morning, where he had provided her with one-to-one feedback on a short story she'd written, as he was doing with each student in the class. Amy's story centred around the time when she was little and she'd let go of a balloon and it had floated off and got stuck up in a tree. She'd climbed up to get it but got stuck up there herself and the fire brigade had to be called. He chuntered away about the themes of childhood and loss, and her impressive use of symbolism. He craned his neck dramatically to look at the clock, told her that the allotted twenty minutes were over and that she could come back at 5.30pm to discuss it further. She was dubious how much more needed discussing but flattered that he deemed her work worthy of further attention. He seemed to her to give everything to his work but was at the same time guarded and aloof. She tried to picture his home life, both he and his wife sitting around with piles of books, reading out amusing extracts to each other. She imagined that his wife was a novelist or a painter, or something equally as impressive.

'Ah, Amy, thank you for coming back. Sorry about earlier, time seems to always get away from me.' He grinned, his midnight-blue shirt rolled up to his elbow. She smiled back, a small closed-mouth smile that she hoped was visible enough.

'Please. Take a seat.'

Amy lowered herself down on a small brown wooden chair and the professor wheeled his over towards her. She caught a whiff of his aftershave, strong and gingery. He flicked through a pile of papers on his lap until he found Amy's.

'Oh yes, the balloon, the tree. It's good, you write well, but you really need to bring out the key themes.' He licked his finger and flicked over to the second page. 'This isn't just a cute story about how you got stuck up a tree. It's more than that, isn't it?'

Is it? Amy thought to herself. 'Yes,' she said softly.

He placed his hand on her knee and looked her in the eye. 'Amy, I want to know how you *felt* up that tree… I want to know how *the balloon* felt up that tree.'

Amy looked down at his hand on her knee, weathered and hairy. *Does he put his hand on everyone's knee? Probably just the girls*, she thought. He moved it off and looked away from her, gazing out the window for a moment, knowing that she was waiting for him to speak. He ran his hand through his immaculately groomed beard. They talked some more about the story, or more accurately, he talked and she listened, breaking eye contact every so often to take down notes in her pad. Aware that he was looking at the page, she made her writing intentionally illegible.

'Amy, I'm having a little soirée at my place this weekend if you fancy it? Just a few of the students I think have the most potential. I'd like you to come,' he said as she packed her stuff away into her bag. 'We sit around reading books and setting the world to rights. If that sounds truly awful, then I understand.' He smiled.

'No, it sounds… interesting,' Amy replied, her stomach lurching at the idea. She looked at the professor, his emerald-green eyes undeniably engaging.

'Good. You're on the system, aren't you? I'll email you the details.'

'Thanks.' Amy nodded, scooping up her bag and heading for the door.

*

Will cut away at some crudely designed artwork with a pair of red Crayola scissors he'd plundered from Izzy's craft drawer and then passed it along to Luke. With a steely eye, Luke folded it and slid it inside the plastic cassette case, before passing it to Pete, who slipped it into a jiffy bag and scrawled out the address in marker pen.

'I'm telling Mum you're using up all the printer ink,' chirped Izzy. She'd reined in the annoying little sister act for a while after Jake had died but had decided that he'd had more than enough respite now.

Will pushed his tongue into his cheek and gurned at her. 'I'm telling Mum you've drunk all the lemonade then,' he said, shutting her up.

The remaining members of SharpShooter had recorded two songs in a day at Kev's studio, the new song 'Pure Love,' and an acoustic track called 'Neon Stranger' that Will had pieced together from lines in Jake's notebook. After much coaxing, Pete had provided backing vocals and they had filled Will's voice out with buckets of reverb until he was just about happy with it. They'd decided to send some demos out to labels, publishers and radio stations in the hopes of gaining some attention again. There was still an indomitable question mark hanging over the band's future, but the trio really believed in these new songs and wanted people to hear them.

Luke folded another label. 'I saw Charlotte's mum the other day. I asked after her. She's doing a bit better apparently. Still pining for Jake, though.'

Will cut steadily along the black line. 'Aren't we all,' he sighed.

One by one, they pulled the adhesive strips off the jiffy bags, stuck them down and stuffed them in an old carrier bag to be sent out.

*

Amy shuffled across campus, her charity-shop chic handbag slung over her shoulder. She passed the library and headed to the post room. Among the ramshackle assortment of parcels, there were two items for her, a care package from her mum containing coffee, flumps and a hardback book. And a letter. She recognised the handwriting immediately, spidery and not yet fully formed – it was Will's. She sat down on a bench opposite the fishpond and opened it with a sense of trepidation.

Dear Amy,

I hope you are enjoying London and are settling into your new place. How are lectures going?

I'm really sorry about everything that happened this summer and how it ended. I had a tough time with Jake and everything, but I shouldn't have lost sight of what I had with you. I'm sorry.

The big news is that Mum is now seeing Jake's dad. I practically caught them at it on the sofa! I've not really got my head around it yet. I don't know, maybe I should accept it, but it just feels weird right now.

We're playing in Islington on 14th November if you fancy coming along? Bring your new uni friends too, I would love to meet them. I'm singing now, so try not to take the piss too much!

Miss you,
Will x

Amy read it slowly, twice. She ran her tongue over her teeth, feeling sad and confused. She had spent the whole summer waiting for Will and now he wanted her back? She put the letter in her inside pocket and headed back to her halls. Kate was in the kitchen making a Thai green curry. She thrust a spoon out at Amy to try some, instructing her to blow on it first. Amy licked some off, fragrant with a bit of heat; she gave it a thumbs-up.

'You want some? There's loads to go around.'

'I'm OK, thanks. I'm out for dinner tonight.'

'Oooh, a date?' Kate beamed.

'Not as such. My English professor is having a thing at his house.'

Kate furrowed her brow. 'Is that legit?'

'I think so. It's not just me, some others from the course will be there.'

Kate stirred the curry in a slow circular motion. 'Is he hot?'

'Urgh. He's like nearly fifty!'

'And…'

'Yeah, kind of.' Amy giggled.

She headed to her room and then showered, letting the jets of warm water wash over her lithe body, pondering what one wears to a soirée. She wrapped a towel around her wet hair and sat down at her desk. She flicked over to a fresh page of her notepad and took a blue fountain pen out from her pencil case.

Dear Will,

Thanks for your letter. Uni is going well, I'm settling in fine and the lectures have been really interesting. I'm looking forward to exploring London more too!

I'm not sure when I will be back next, but I will try and make your gig next month. It's great that you are keeping the band going — all the best with it.

Jake's dad seemed like a nice guy. He's never going to replace your dad, you know that, but your mum has also had a hard time. They both deserve some happiness. They aren't doing it to upset you. Try and accept it, it would make you the bigger person here.

I hope we can still be friends.

Amy

She read it over and folded it neatly into an envelope, ready to drop into the post room the following day. She finished getting ready, applying her favourite purple eyeshadow, pairing it with a green floral dress that she hoped was both bookish and stylish. She took a swig of vodka and headed off campus.

After getting off the bustling tube at Holborn, she walked down the grotty high street, dusty with litter and heavy with traffic. She stopped at a newsagents to get a bottle of wine, pushing the boat out to break the six-pound mark. She clutched the piece of paper with the professor's address tightly in her right hand, arriving at a quaint block of flats with a big wooden double door. At 7.30pm exactly she buzzed number 6 and the professor let her in.

'Ah, Amy, good to see you. Come on in, take your jacket off. You're the first one here actually,' he said, gesturing towards the living room. It was small, with multiple shelves crammed with books, ornaments of various origins and paintings of conflicting aesthetics.

'I brought some wine,' said Amy, handing it to him.

The professor inspected the label with a thinly concealed smile. 'New Zealand. Thank you.' He was wearing a white thick-cotton shirt and beige turned-up chinos, his hair slicked back with Brylcreem. 'Sit down,' he said, pointing to an armchair. 'I'm making chicken with potato gratin. I hope you're not veggie. I forgot to ask.'

Amy fiddled with her left earring, dangly ones she didn't wear often. 'No, sounds good. Thanks.'

'I've got a few writing exercises and things lined up. I think we're in for a pretty lively evening,' said the professor, pouring lashings of balsamic vinegar on the salad.

As the evening passed, Amy found herself clinging to the professor's every word as he spun yarns about his university days and teaching English in South Korea in his early twenties. He had no children, he told her, but said nothing of his wife, other than that she was away with work a lot.

When dinner was ready, it became apparent to Amy that no one else was coming. He told her that four others had accepted the invite, but that they must have had better offers. Amy wasn't sure if she believed him, he certainly hadn't made enough food for six people, but she probed no further. The food was rich with flavour and served with plenty of wine, but not Amy's, which remained firmly in the fridge.

After dinner, he'd surprised her by skinning up and offering her some. She'd wondered if it was a test at first, but he assured her that all the creatives smoked and it was really no big deal. They shared a joint and chatted gushingly about TS Eliot and Sylvia Plath. Sometime later, when conversation stalled, he leant over and kissed her. His beard was brittle and scratchy, but his lips soft and more youthful than she'd imagined.

'Is that OK?' he asked.

Amy nodded, saying nothing.

'Let's go to the bedroom,' he whispered.

Amy followed him down the hall to the bedroom, unsure of what she was doing, her vision foggy and head feeling floaty. His room was impossibly neat and organised, with a thin woollen blanket on top of the duvet.

'Your wife?' Amy asked.

'She's OK with it. We have a kind of open relationship,' he said, kissing her again. They lay down on the bed together; he took off his trousers and asked her to give him oral, which she did, for a minute or so, before pulling away. The sex that followed was rough and dispassionate. Amy tried to look into his eyes, but he kept them firmly shut as he grunted away. He shuddered to an end and turned away on his side. Amy lay there for a while, staring at the ceiling, her head spinning, before passing out.

When she awoke the next morning, the professor was up and dressed, pacing around the room.

'You have to leave,' he said, not looking at her.

Amy rubbed her eyes and stretched her arms out above her head. 'Can I get a coffee first?'

He handed Amy her clothes. 'No time, sorry.'

Amy dressed hastily, shoving her tights in her bag. The professor kissed her swiftly on the cheek but did not look her in the eye as she left.

*

The early-afternoon sun tried to prise its way through the clouds, Amy sat on the bed of her dorm, knees up under her chest. Through her window she could hear a group of boys throwing a Frisbee around on the lawn. Kate had asked her if she wanted to grab lunch somewhere in central together, but she didn't feel like it.

She sat there trying to process what had happened the night before. The experience had not been entirely unpleasant, at all times she was aware of what she was doing, albeit through a haze of wine and weed, yet she felt dirty and used. She thought about George, who predictably she'd not heard from, and about when she was sixteen and

199

she'd had sex with Scott Newman in his car. Afterwards, he'd thrown her out and she'd had to walk home in the rain. She was sure that she deserved better than this. Eventually, she showered, washing the professor's scent off her, before heading to the library to check her emails. Among the campus newsletters and reading-list emails was a new one from 'Prof J Walker'.

> *Amy,*
>
> *Thanks for coming last night, I hope you enjoyed it as much as I did. Let's do it again some time :)*
>
> *Jeremy*

CHAPTER 31

Will, Pete and Luke sat quietly in the Corsa, crammed in amongst cymbal stands, guitar cases and battered cardboard boxes of CDs. Horns beeped and angry drivers mouthed off at each other as they crawled through the London rush-hour traffic.

'Did many people get back to you about the CDs you sent out?' asked Luke.

Will rested his arm on a guitar amp and leaned forward to reply. 'A couple. I've put Tim from Universal on the guestlist for this evening.'

'That's awesome,' said Pete, flicking on the radio, the exuberant drive-time presenter unable to resist talking over the songs.

Eventually they arrived in Islington and loaded their gear into the venue via a back-alley entrance that reeked of piss. SharpShooter were third on a four-band bill, as part of *Rock the City '97*. The promo pack had promised that a plethora of managers, agents, publishers, radio-pluggers and A&R scouts would all be at the event, looking for the next big thing. They had just twenty-five minutes to impress.

Will felt seasick at the idea of singing main vocals for the first time. Rehearsals had gone well, but nothing could really prepare for a gig – the lights, the crowd, the tendency for equipment to stop working for no reason. His nerves were amplified by the notion that they had a proper record label coming specifically to watch them. When he thought back to their first rehearsal, to Miss Howard telling them to turn everything down or they wouldn't be able to use the room again, it didn't seem possible that this was where they were now.

Luke and Pete went to fetch a kebab from a nearby dive, but Will felt too queasy. He stayed in the venue alone, watching the first band, constantly checking that his lucky plectrum was still in his back pocket. He swigged from a can of flat lager and hoped that the room would soon fill up. He missed Jake more than ever now. He hadn't realised how much his energy and confidence helped to propel him along, to vaporise his lingering doubts. He tried not to think about Amy, and whether she would show up or not. For days he had obsessed about the way she signed off her letter with 'I hope we can be friends', with no kiss at the end. Did 'friends' mean there was no way back? He didn't want to be friends; he wanted all of her.

As Pete and Luke arrived back at the venue, the second band, The Rays, took to the stage. The majority of the audience seemed to be there for them, whooping and cheering, surging closer to the stage. The singer sauntered across the stage in oversized sunglasses, spouting phrases like, '*Y'all having a good time?*' and, '*Let me see those hands in the air,'* like he was an action figure with a pull string in his back. The boys stood at the back with their arms folded while The Rays stormed through a set of funky, good-time party music – something SharpShooter most definitely were not. Will noticed a punter pick up one of the new SharpShooter flyers he'd had printed from the bar. Buoyed that someone was taking an interest, he homed in as the chap took a cursory glance, spat his chewing gum out, folded it up inside and put it back on the bar, instantly deflating Will's heart.

'The crowd are loving it,' he said anxiously, nodding over to the stage.

'Yeah, this kind of stuff is fine live, but no label is going to want to put that out,' Luke reassured.

The Rays' indulgent set over-ran massively and they chatted casually with friends as they slowly packed up their gear. Will stood by the side of the stage, sweaty-palmed and eager to get set up before the audience evaporated. There was no sign of the A&R rep from Universal, but there was a healthy crowd by now – he tried to focus on that. His hands trembled as he tuned his guitar and set up his FX pedals, linking them one by one with great care. They had barely finished setting up when the house music stopped and the lights went up, casting an eerie silence over the venue. Will looked at Pete and Luke; they nodded in unison.

'For Jake,' said Luke quietly, clicking his sticks together four times.

The three of them locked tightly into 'No Love Lost'.

'Just keep moving and the sadness won't find you,' Will sang, his voice rebounding back at him in the monitors; the song gliding along elegantly. During the outro, however,

Pete's bass began to crackle and pop. He stopped to turn his amp down, losing his place as the song tripped over the line to muted applause. Will looked out at the audience, just about making out their shadowy faces through the glare of the lights. No Amy.

'Thank you,' he stammered, introducing the next song. He was relieved it was a faster, heavier one; there was always more margin for error with that type of number – duff notes could be buried under the noise, and vocals shouted, not sung. During the final chorus, his microphone cut out and a portly soundman scampered on stage to change the lead. Will glared at him in a manner he hoped wasn't too diva-ish but still portrayed that he was royally pissed off. His fingers jangled as he began the intricate arpeggio of 'Pure Love'. This was the first time they'd played it live and the crowd burbled away, drowning out the delicate intro, agitating him further.

'*You showed me the lights, you showed me the sights, showed me everything good in life,*' he sang, noticeable off-key. '*And tonight, I'll raise a glass, to a life, cut short by the past.*' He wavered, feeling his throat begin to tighten and constrict. He looked to his right where Jake should have been, then out at the audience where Amy was not, and felt his eyes begin to fill with tears.

Unable to focus, he fluffed his guitar part and missed the next vocal. Luke and Pete looked at him for cues on when to change, but he avoided their eyes. They moved to the chorus, yet still no words came. Will squatted down on his haunches and stopped playing, the buzzing in his ears drowning out his thoughts and vision dissolving to nothing. Pete and Luke ploughed on for a few more bars, before collapsing to a stop.

Will laid his guitar down on the stage floor to a howl of feedback, his breathing sharp and erratic. 'I'm sorry, I can't do this,' he said into the microphone. Pete took off his bass and helped him to his feet, feeling the eyes of the audience on them. Their murmuring had stopped now and they stood silent, arms folded, watching the car crash unfold in front of them.

'Come on, mate, you can do it,' Pete said softly.

Will was full-on sobbing now, a bubble of snot bulging from his left nostril, his face contorting as if he was standing on hot coals. He shook his head frantically left to right.

'I can't. I'm sorry.'

Pete helped him from the stage like a mountain rescuer escorting a rambler with a twisted ankle. Luke unscrewed his cymbals and swiftly followed suit.

The promoter raced down to the side of the stage to meet them.

'What the hell's going on?'

'He's not well enough to continue,' said Pete.

'What am I supposed to do?'

'Just put the next band on. No one will care,' Luke snapped.

'OK, but you lot aren't getting paid.'

'Is that all you care about?' Luke rebutted.

With that, the promoter indicated to the soundman to put the house music on, and he obliged with some inoffensive acid jazz. Pete and Luke cleared the stage of their gear, while Will sat backstage sipping on some water, cradling it in his hands, trying desperately to compose himself, his head like candyfloss.

The car ride home was largely silent. As they approached the outskirts of Malford, Will apologised for letting them all down and the others accepted it with good grace, pretending it was no big deal, when in truth they were gutted.

The estate was eerily quiet, the streetlights casting it in amber. Pete pulled up outside Will's and opened the door for him. 'Are you sure you're OK?'

'Yeah, I'm all right,' said Will, levering himself out of the car. 'It just all got a bit much.'

'Try and get some sleep, mate.'

Will nodded gently, a sad, resigned gesture, before heading towards the house. He passed Elmo, licking his paws on the driveway, but he looked away, as if even he was disappointed in him.

CHAPTER 32

Will,

Sorry I didn't make your show, I had a ton of uni work to do. Hope it went well?

I heard from Charlotte that you've been going out running and are working in the cafe now, that's great, keep it up!

Amy

P.S. You should get on email, it's all the rage these days and would save us on stamps!

Amy dropped the letter in the post box and continued down the street towards the station. She stood waiting outside it, shielding herself from the rain with a black polka-dot umbrella. Charlotte was coming to stay for the weekend and every couple of minutes, as a new wave of people passed through the turnstiles, Amy would crane her neck to see if she was one of them. It would be the first time they'd seen each other since the summer. She felt like so much had happened since then, like Malford was nothing but a memory, that maybe she hadn't really existed there at all. A few minutes later, Charlotte came bounding out of the station, covering her head with her bag as the cold rain continued to lash down. Amy waved frantically, greeting her with a soggy embrace.

Charlotte grabbed a pack of fags from her jacket and lit up. 'So, what's the plan?' she asked, her mouth wrapped round a cigarette.

'Get home, get dry. There's a thing on at the SU bar tonight. I've signed you in for it.'

Charlotte linked arms with Amy and they weaved through the hordes of people, away from the station. They hopped on a bus back to campus. It meandered through the traffic, stopping every hundred yards to let sour-faced people on or off. Amy watched two raindrops chase each other down the windowpane as they chatted freely on the upper deck. Charlotte, clearly still hurting, talked about Jake, and Amy listened with genuine compassion.

Over a makeshift dinner of jacket potato and baked beans, Amy introduced Charlotte to her roommates Kate, Emily and Saskia. They probed her about what Amy was like at school and Charlotte remained tight-lipped, unsure of what they were hoping she'd say. After they'd eaten, the two of them got ready to go out in Amy's room, the dirty guitars of *Celebrity Skin* competing with the noise of the hairdryer. They shared a bottle of Lambrini, warm and sickly sweet, as they applied their makeup and picked out their outfits.

'So, you seeing anyone here yet?' asked Charlotte.

'Kind of. I'm not sure, really.'

'Go on…'

Amy pressed her fingers to her lips. 'I can't say any more.'

'Why not?'

'He's a little older than me.'

'Mature student – nice.'

'Not exactly,' said Amy, sheepishly.

'Not a teacher?'

Amy said nothing.

'Don't tell me you are shagging a teacher!'

Amy blushed. 'Professor, actually.'

'Amy!' Charlotte shrieked in mock horror. 'You have to tell me everything... and I mean *everything*.'

'Later. You can't say anything, though.'

'My lips are sealed.' Charlotte laughed, pursing her blood-red lips together.

Since the dinner party that wasn't a dinner party, Amy had seen Professor Walker twice. Once at his place when his wife was out at the theatre, and then at an after-hours session in his office. They communicated solely by email, but she found herself thinking about him all the time, searching the library computer for everything she could find about him, obsessing over tiny details and wishing she could speak to him whenever she wanted. She'd still not heard from George, but he seemed so young and pointless compared to the professor: a boy, not a man.

The SU was heaving; there was a charity auction of the football team on where students could bid for the chance to go on dates with them. Amy knew it was narcissistic, and borderline sexist, but justified it to herself as a bit of fun for a good cause. 'There She Goes' jangled out from the jukebox as the pair sat down at a table by the window. They ordered two Southern Comfort and lemonades from the ridiculously cheap bar, lit a cigarette each and sat catching up. The team captain Lee Prichard was the star attraction at the auction, with a girl from the hockey team bidding £30 for a dinner date with him that seemed unlikely to ever happen.

Half an hour later, Charlotte went to the bar for more drinks. Amy sat waiting for her to come back with them. She sucked on a cigarette and peered through the throng of people to see if she was OK, spotting her at the bar, a guy in her ear. Amy recognised the back of that head – thick brown hair and strong neck – it was George. He brushed Charlotte's bare shoulder with his hand, and Charlotte, arms folded across her chest, said something to make him step back. He smiled widely, over-compensating, and continued to chirps her. Amy watched on, a pang of jealously in her stomach. She contemplated going over but decided against it. Eventually, Charlotte came back, clutching their drinks.

'You OK?' asked Amy.

'Yeah, sorry, I got talking to a guy at the bar. Bit of a prick.'

'I know.' Amy smiled.

When the bar called time, they joined Amy's dormmates Kate, Emily and Saskia at a small basement club a short, drunken walk away. The Union Jack-style poster on the door promised to play the best of British pop. They slid over three pound coins each for entrance.

After navigating the narrow death-trap stairs, they knocked back some shots at the bar: a tequila and a luminous appley concoction. Down on the dancefloor, the DJ whacked out 'Tainted Love' and 'Just Can't Get Enough' in quick succession as the girls spun around, singing along joyously. A lanky, greasy-haired boy approached them, barging his way through a group of lads on the periphery.

'You made it!' shouted Saskia over the music. 'Guys, this is Jack – he's on my course,' she said, turning to the others. The group waved back indifferently. Jack cavorted away to the music in the centre of the group, before singling out Amy and moving closer to speak in her ear.

'Would you care to dance with me?' he asked, unfurling his arm in a knowingly old-fashioned way.

'I'm OK, thanks,' replied Amy, her head spinning from the potent combination of loud music and cheap alcohol.

Jack purposely left his hand out, dangling in limbo. 'You sure?'

'Totally,' replied Amy.

'Suit yourself,' scoffed Jack, as he slunk off to the bar.

Saskia scowled at her through the dry ice. 'You didn't have to be rude to him, Amy. He's a good guy.'

'I wasn't. I just didn't want to dance with him.'

'Why not? Too young for you?'

The other girls guffawed loudly.

'Piss off!' snapped Amy, flouncing off to the toilets. She had told Kate about the professor in confidence, yet now everyone seemed to know. Their laughter was loaded with bile; she could sense it. She locked herself in the cubicle and began to cry – big salty tears that made her makeup run in thick, inky-black trails. She clawed at the roll of toilet paper and tried to wipe her face clean. She didn't want to go back out there. She knew they would all be talking about her, sharing invented details of her sordid relationship.

A while later, she composed herself and poked her head out from the toilets. As she tentatively re-emerged, she could make out Charlotte joking around with the others on the dancefloor and instantly felt betrayed. She stormed out of the club and slumped down against the outside wall, her head thumping. The rain was lashing down again now and her dress began to soak through as she sat on the filthy pavement. She needed to see the professor. He was the only one who truly understood her. She could walk it from here in twenty minutes, she reasoned.

An hour later, she stumbled up to his apartment block, her pumps squelching and dress sodden. She pushed the buzzer firmly with her dripping-wet finger. Eventually, the professor opened the door in a dressing gown, his hair dishevelled and barely open eyes reminiscent of a new-born mouse. His drowsy face changed to one of pure disdain the moment he saw who it was.

'Jesus Christ, Amy. What are you doing here?' he whispered.

'I wanted to see you.'

He shook his head. 'Well, you can't.'

'Don't be like that,' Amy slurred.

'I'm not being like anything. It's just not convenient right now,' he hushed, indicating towards the house.

'I've fallen out with my friends and I need somewhere to stay.'

The professor looked at her clearly for the first time, her eyes big black smudges and hair matted tangles.

'Well, you can't stay here. I'll give you the money for a taxi.'

'Who is it, darling? Everything OK?' came a voice from inside the house.

'Just kids messing around. It's OK, I'll get rid of them,' he shouted back.

The professor put his finger to his lips and scurried off into the house. He came back with a flimsy £20 note and handed it to Amy. She snatched it from him silently. She wanted so badly to scream out, to let his wife know that she was here, but knew that she couldn't. She looked at him for a second and then turned and left without saying a word.

After several failed attempts, she eventually flagged down a black cab. She zoned out as the cabbie banged on about the traffic and his own daughter being away at university. Her head echoed with the professor's words, *'I'll get rid of her.'* The next thing she remembered was struggling with her door key, collapsing through the door and passing out on her bed.

The next morning, she woke up bleary-eyed and slowly tried to piece together the night before. *Shit, where's Charlotte?*

She tip-toed gingerly down the hall to find her on the sofa in the common room, nursing a cup of tea.

'What the fuck happened to you last night?' she said, shaking her head.

Amy swept her morning hair out of her eyes. 'Don't ask.'

Charlotte said nothing, just looked at her expectantly.

'I'm so sorry. Did the others get you home OK?' Amy asked.

'Yeah. They were all saying you were a complete bitch for leaving me, though.'

'Is that what you think too?'

'I'm on the fence about it.' She smiled.

'I'm sorry, I just got too wasted. I'm so glad you're OK.'

Amy sat down beside her and put her head on Charlotte's shoulder. Her mind flickered between a flashback of the professor's face, rugged and handsome, and Will's, fresh and boyish. She shut her eyes in an attempt to erase them both and fell asleep.

CHAPTER 33

The café staff room smelt of a curious mix of coffee and eggs. The kettle was boiling and Radio 2 played away to no one in particular. Yesterday's unsold baked goods sat on the work surface, free for the taking. Will took a sip from his carton of orange juice, took a pen and pad out from his rucksack, and began to write to Amy. He could feel himself being jettisoned from her life, seemingly powerless to stop it, but he had to try.

Dear Amy,

The gig was an absolute disaster! I'll spare you the details, but let's just say I realised too late that we couldn't do it without Jake.

I have been running, yes! I still can't go far without getting a stitch, though. The café is pretty boring, but I'm feeling a little better now, generally. I've been seeing a counsellor (a bloke called Simon), which is helping. I guess I just feel a bit left behind, like everyone has gone off to uni and I'm still stuck here.

Let me know if you are coming back for Christmas – it would be great to see you again.

Will

P.S. – I have heard of email, thanks! I'm on at Mum to get the internet and then I'll get one sorted.

He tore the letter out of his notepad and stuffed it into an envelope before he could change his mind.

'Will, can we talk?' said Chloe, entering the room.

Will hastily threw the envelope in his bag and gestured for her to sit down opposite him.

'What happened between us. I'm not sure if you're embarrassed or what, but I feel like you've been avoiding me since,' said Chloe, taking a seat.

'Sorry,' said Will softly.

'It was just a drunken hook-up, no big deal,' whispered Chloe.

Will looked up at her, loosening up slightly. 'I do like you, Chloe, just not really in that way. Sorry.'

Chloe shuffled in her seat.

Will pointed at his tuna sandwich on the table. 'Would you like the other half of this? I have no appetite these days.'

'Sure.'

He slid the plate across the table to her.

'I hope we can still be friends. We are both stuck in this place, we may as well get along,' she said, taking a bite.

Will smiled. 'Friends it is.'

*

When his shift ended, Will headed out to The Griffin to meet Luke and Pete. It was bitterly cold out, the howling wind battled with the incessant ringing in his ears as he lumbered into town wrapped up in his army-green parka. He'd not seen either of them since the *Rock the City* fiasco and they were keen to discuss what was happening next with the band. He posted the letter to Amy on the way, hovering it over the precipice of the post-box window for a few seconds before committing himself to letting it go. Letters were all he had left of her and each one was like a small piece of himself being sent away to war.

When he arrived at the pub, the others were already there, sitting at a small table in the corner next to the artificial Christmas tree, draped in gold tinsel and gaudy plastic baubles. He picked up a Strongbow from the bar and went over to join them. He shook their hands firmly. He'd been told before that his handshake was too limp but didn't understand why so much importance was placed on such trivial things.

'Want some crisps?' asked Luke. 'It's a *Sheffield Shuffle.*'

'What's that?'

'It's when you get two different flavours and mix them together.'

'Yeah, I don't think that's a real thing.' Will laughed.

They made small talk for a few minutes before Will decided to face the elephant in the room head on.

'I'm really sorry about the gig, guys. I let you both down… I let myself down.'

Luke stared at the table, unable to meet his eye. 'It's OK. Maybe we pushed you too hard.'

Will watched the bubbles in his drink rising to the top for a moment. 'It seems so silly to me now, but at the time...' His voice trailed off.

'We've been thinking,' said Pete, helping him out. 'We don't think we should continue without a new singer.'

Will exhaled. 'I agree.'

'But we also don't think it's worth the hassle of getting a new singer, because, and I'm sorry to drop this on you like this, we've both applied for uni in the summer.'

Will felt a sadness thump him in the chest; he took a swig of his drink and remained silent.

Pete scratched his nose with his fingernail. 'We'll always have the songs, and the memories, but we just feel like it's time to, you know, get on with our lives.'

'Which uni?' asked Will, eventually.

'We've both been accepted at Nottingham,' replied Luke, meeting Will's eye this time.

'It's one of the best in the country for engineering,' added Pete superfluously.

Will unfolded his arms and tried to make sense of what he was hearing.

'Obviously you can come and visit as much as you like,' said Luke.

'But we think you should apply for one too,' added Pete. 'You can't stay in Malford forever.'

Will ripped at the corner of a soggy beer mat, trying to process it all. He'd only ever wanted to be a musician; he had no back-up plan. His tutor had suggested he pursue something in the media, but eighteen felt like too young to be giving up on the dream already. 'Thanks, but I've no idea what I want to do,' he said eventually.

'Well, think about it, mate, you're too good for this place,' said Luke.

Will took another swig of cider and put the glass down on the coaster. 'Some lucky bastards are going to have the best rhythm section in Nottingham.'

Luke and Pete grinned at each other. Will fidgeted in his seat, the hard wooden slats digging into his back. 'We got an answerphone message from XFM yesterday, by the way. The machine's playing up a bit, but the gist of it was they are playing "Pure Love" tomorrow night… for what it's worth.'

'No way. That's awesome!' said Luke.

'Course it's worth something – we are getting played on the radio, no one can ever take that away from us!' said Pete.

Luke lit a cigarette. 'You can both come over to mine, listen to it together if you like?'

Pete nodded. 'I'll drink to that.'

With that, the three of them raised their glasses and clinked them together. Will lowered his arm slowly and downed what was left of his cider, uncertain of everything.

*

Amy lay on her bed, curtains drawn, shutting out the winter gloom. The novel she was reading depicted a scene in a Tuscan vineyard and for a moment she allowed herself to be there – somewhere warmer, somewhere more carefree. She and the other girls on her floor were no longer speaking. Since their night out with Charlotte they had become increasingly unpleasant about the situation with the professor, their comments more and more barbed. This had led to a passive-aggressive Post-It note war on the fridge and some of her possessions being hidden.

Charlotte tried to assure her that they were probably just jealous and that it would blow over in time, but Amy wasn't so sure. One night, she descended into tears and called her parents. She couldn't tell them the reason why there were fighting, only that they weren't getting on at all. They suggested she asked to be moved to another block. Accommodation services said that this was not possible, though. So, after an internal dispute, her father had agreed to subsidise the rent for her own bedsit flat in the new year.

Until then, she planned to keep her head down, confining herself to her room and concentrating on her assignments. Besides lectures, she had seen the professor only once since her uninvited visit. He had invited her over to his place when his wife was out at a gallery opening and they'd had rushed sex before Amy got the bus home. In his lectures she found herself staring at him, trying to catch his eye, but he never looked her way. She put her hand up to answer questions, but he never chose her to answer, over-compensating in case anyone accused him of favouritism. She wished that the other students in the room knew what they had between them but was at the same time mortified by the idea of anyone else finding out.

Her daydreaming was rudely interrupted by the doorbell. She wasn't expecting anyone, so let one of the other girls get the door.

'Amy, it's for you,' shouted Saskia bluntly.

Amy sprang up from the bed and rushed to the door. She was confronted by a blonde-haired woman in her mid to late forties, dark roots peeking through, makeup powdery and excessive.

'Are you Amy Stevens?' she asked without greeting.

'Yes. Can I help you?' said Amy cautiously.

The woman stepped into the hallway, her face uncomfortably close to Amy's, her eyes heavy with emotion. Amy tried to step back, but before she could she felt a fierce smack to the face.

'Stay away from my husband! OK?'

Amy lifted her hand to her cheek, it burnt red as the pain dispersed through it. *Professor Walker's wife.*

Hot tears stung her eyes; she tried to blink them clear but couldn't.

'If I find out you've been to the house again, you little slut, I'll finish you. Understand?'

Amy tried to make sense of it all, her head pounding. 'Get out,' she mustered weakly.

Coloured shapes spun in her vision as she slammed the door shut behind her. Her breathing shallow and rapid, she let herself slide down the wall to the floor. With her head in her hands, she began to sob. She blubbed in a manner she hadn't done since junior school, when a girl had spat gum in her hair and she'd had to have it cut out. Her cheek still burning and throat constricting, she sat slumped on the hallway carpet. She knew the other girls must have heard the commotion, and part of her hoped that they would come and see if she was OK, but no one did.

CHAPTER 34

Will's sweaty hands clung to the PlayStation controller as Lara Croft waded through the shallow, murky water. He skilfully avoided some falling rocks, her triangular breasts bobbing just above the surface. His door was ajar and he could hear his mum on the phone. She was chatting warmly and laughing – something he'd not heard for a long time. He paused the game to listen in and deduced it was Mick on the other end.

'Will's out tonight, so I can come over, as long as you don't mind me bringing Izzy?'

Frustrated that he couldn't hear the other end of the conversation, he considered picking up the cordless to listen in but thought better of it.

'You know, I like you… we just need to take it slow. Izzy is excited about it all… I'm just not sure about Will yet.'

Mick must have made some kind of quip because she laughed again, loud and affectionately. She sounded genuinely happy, like she used to, before Dad died. Will un-paused the PlayStation. Amy's words about being the bigger person circled around his head, and he had the crushing realisation that he was being selfish. *Why shouldn't she have someone that makes her smile?* Just because he was miserable most of the time didn't mean everyone around him had to be. When he was certain she'd hung up the phone, he ambled downstairs and stopped her in the kitchen.

'Mum, I was thinking—'

'There's a first.'

'I'm serious.'

'Sorry.'

'I was thinking, if you wanted to invite Mick over for Christmas, you know, then that would be OK with me.'

Helen looked at him with grateful eyes. She moved towards him and put her arms around him. 'Really, love?'

'Yeah, I guess.' He shrugged, his face flush with scarlet.

'Thank you,' she said, kissing him on the forehead. 'I mean, I'll have to ask him, he might already have plans, but that's very kind of you.' Helen filled the kettle and flicked it on. 'Would you like a cuppa?'

'No, I'm good,' replied Will, anxious to escape back to his room.

'There's some post on the table for you, by the way.'

Will snatched it up quickly and looked at it with a shiver of disappointment. The address was typed, not handwritten, meaning it wasn't from Amy. He stuffed it in the front pocket of his hoodie and took it upstairs. He sat down on his bed, put his thumb under the lip of the envelope and levered it open.

Dear Will,

Thank you for putting me on the guestlist for your show at Rock the City last month. I'm sorry that it didn't go as planned for you. I spoke to your bass player on the night and he explained the situation with your singer, so I fully understand and would like to pass on my condolences to you and his family.

I still love the demo and was impressed with the songs I did hear live. While I don't see the band as a signable option right now, I passed the CD on to my colleague in our publishing arm and I am delighted to say that they would like to offer you a place on our Young Songwriters course starting in London in the new year, should you be interested, of course.

The syllabus is run in association with Haringey College and they will be in touch in the next few days with all the details. Obviously, it's totally up to you, but it's a great opportunity and the tutors are some of the best songwriters in the business.

Kind regards,
Tim Bradshaw
Universal Records

Yes! A giddy wave of excitement rushed through him. He read the letter over and over again. He thought about London, the prospect of getting out of Malford, of being closer to Amy, his mind racing to make arrangements, a gormless smile plastered on his face. He stuffed the letter in his coat pocket; he could not wait to show the others.

*

Amy sat cross-legged on her bedroom floor running the hairdryer over her hair. It was taking every fibre of her being not to go to the library and email the professor. She thought about him, his hairy torso, strong arms and rugged face. *How did his wife find out?* It really didn't matter, yet she cared immensely for the answer all the same.

Out in the common room, Emily, Saskia and Kate were cooking together, jabbering away loudly. She flicked her radio on in an attempt to drown them out and laid down on her bed, cradling a cuddly toy in her arms. It was the penguin that 'Will' had won her in Dorset. She clutched it tightly to her chest, stroking its soft yellow beak. The sprawling outro of 'Bitter Sweet Symphony' was interrupted by an abrasive sting for XFM New Music Mondays.

'Up next we've got a new band called SharpShooter,' said the presenter. Amy sat up sharply, dropping the penguin to the floor. She turned to face the radio, unsure of why she did so; it wasn't a TV.

'A three-piece from Malford, they describe themselves as a cross between Sonic Youth and Radiohead, which got me interested, for sure, and this song is called "Pure Love".'

The opening riff chimed out of the radio, tinny but melodic, a sweeping cinematic quality to it.

'*You showed me the lights, you showed me the sights, Showed me everything good in life.*'

Amy listened closely to the voice, fragile and drenched in reverb. It wasn't Jake's, *it was Will's.*

A shiver passed through her body. The drums and bass kicked in fully, pouring from the speakers.

'*Pure love, of that I am glad, but I'm missing the future we once had,*' sang Will, his voice belonging to another life.

Amy smiled, a hushed expressionless smudge of a smile. A solitary tear trailed down her cheek.

'*Fragments of youth, fragments of joy, for every girl and every boy. And as the curtain calls, we'll take a bow. Nothing is forever, but forever is now.*'

She grabbed the penguin again and squeezed it against her, smiling widely now as the song faded to an end.

'How good was that?!' exclaimed the presenter. Amy re-ran Will's words through her head; heartfelt and vulnerable. She rifled through her drawer and found *Fragments of Youth*, the mixtape that he had made for her when they'd first begun dating. She had listened to it to death at the time, but it had lain untouched in her drawer for some time now. It felt surreal to hear it referenced on national radio, like their little in-joke was being broadcast to the world. She shut her eyes and thought about him – the youthful, flawed features of his face and boyish curls still clear in her mind. She thought about the professor, his wife, the mark on her cheek that she was still covering with concealer. There was no future in that; she would be kidding herself if she thought otherwise.

She decided that she urgently needed to speak to Will, to tell him that she'd heard his song, and that, just maybe, she missed him. She grabbed some change from the old jam jar in her room, threw on a jacket and bounded across the campus to the payphone outside the library. The lawn was frosted over and her breath visible in the air as she tried to recall his home phone number. She slid a twenty-pence coin into the payphone slot, followed by two tens, and pushed down the cold metal buttons.

The phone rang, no answer. It rang again, for a fourth, fifth and sixth time. *Come on, come on, answer the phone.*

She wasn't sure exactly what she was going to say, or whether he'd be pleased to hear from her, but at that moment it felt right. The phone rang three more times, before making a clunky clicking sound.

'Hello, this is the Green household.' Helen's voice. 'Please leave a message after the tone.' There was an elongated bleep. Amy contemplated hanging up, before deciding to leave a message. He couldn't speak back this way; she could just say what she needed to say, and it would be up to him if he wanted to call her back or see her again. Another clicking sound interrupted her as she went to speak. Amy ignored it, took a deep breath and composed herself.

'Hi, Will, it's Amy. Um, you must not be in, but I was just calling to say that I heard your song on the radio, and that I loved it, and that… um… I'm proud of you.' She swapped the receiver from her left hand to her right. 'Anyway, I will be back at Christmas, if you want to hang out or something.' Her voice trembled in the air.

'I miss you.'

Amy slammed the receiver down before she could ramble on or begin to cry. She pulled her hood up tightly over her head and headed back to her halls. She needed sleep.

*

Helen turned her key in the door and wiped her feet on the mat. 'Will,' she called out. No response. As she kicked off her shoes, she heard the answerphone beeping in the bedroom and went through to see who it was. She pushed down the big white play button with her index finger. The machine beeped, a rustling sound played for a moment, before going dead. She dialled 1471. It was a London number she didn't recognise.

They'll call back if it's important.

CHAPTER 35

Three weeks later – Christmas Eve 1997

Amy gripped the handrail tightly as the train chuntered along, a wheelie case stuffed full of clothes clasped between her knees. It was cold outside, barely a couple of degrees, but the carriage was roasting with body heat. She wanted to take her jacket off but lacked the room for such a manoeuvre. 'Pictures of You' blared away in her headphones; she stared out the window at the passing countryside and imagined she was in a film. She hadn't been back to Malford since September. She was looking forward to seeing her parents again but knew they would inevitably drive her crazy after a couple of days.

Amy struggled towards the door of the train and a balding man in a brown donkey jacket helped her with her case. She thanked him profusely and turned to see Roger and Margaret standing either side of their white Mazda in the car park. Margaret waved frantically as she approached.

Amy returned the wave briefly, turning her head backwards and pretending to check the wheels of her case were running properly, the shame she felt about her first term making it difficult to meet their eye. As she reached them, Margaret engulfed her in a loving hug. Roger hopped uneasily from foot to foot beside them, anxious to get going 'before the weather set in'.

The short drive home was prolonged by the heavy Christmas traffic. Roger searched through the radio stations, each one of them seemingly obliged to play Chris Rea; the jaunty rhythm at odds with his gravelly voice as sleet began to pepper the car.

'How was your journey?' he asked.

'Yeah, fine,' replied Amy. She knew that he wanted to know more detail – the changes on the tube, the conditions on the train – but she was too tired to indulge him.

'How's your course?' asked Margaret.

'It's all right. I don't really feel like I'm being stretched that much, though, to be honest.'

Margaret thought this was a terribly pretentious thing to say but decided not to challenge it. 'Are things better with your roommates?' she asked instead.

'Nope, they're still bitches.'

'Amy!'

'What? They are.' She shrugged.

'So, you still want to move into the flat then?'

'Yes, please,' said Amy, momentarily undoing her seatbelt to finally take her jacket off.

She had not told her mother about the professor, naturally, and planned to avoid the subject of boys, or men rather, altogether for the next week or so. Back at the house, Margaret laid the table and prepared the ham she'd left cooking for supper. Amy tucked into it in a manner which made her mum wonder if she had been eating at all while she was away. She looked thinner than before, her visible collarbone accentuated by the silver chain necklace draped over it. Before bed, the three of them shared a cup of Ovaltine together. Roger lit the fireplace, something he did only a handful of times a year – the smell instantly transporting Amy back to simpler times – and they watched an old Morecambe and Wise Christmas Special. Her parents roared with laughter and Amy didn't have the heart to tell them she thought it hadn't aged well. As an only child, she'd enjoyed having her parents' undivided attention when she was young, but these days she wished she had a sibling – some company, as well as someone to act as a buffer between them and her.

After her parents had gone to bed, Amy stayed up flicking through channels for a bit, before giving in and going up to bed just before midnight. Her room still looked the same; like a relic from a former life. She'd become knowingly ambivalent towards Christmas in recent years but still felt a childlike twinge of excitement as she climbed into bed, pulling the duvet tightly over her and shutting her eyes. Thoughts of Will drifted into her brain, swirling around, lingering uninvited.

Why hasn't he returned my call?

*

It was early morning Christmas Day; a thin frost laced the ground outside. Will perched on the edge of the sofa and watched on as Izzy ripped the shiny red and green paper off a large rectangular present. She hopped madly on the spot as a garish pink SodaStream revealed itself. He admired her sense of wonder, as if she had not yet been blemished by life in the way he had.

'Those things are naff,' said Will.

'Are not,' Izzy replied, sticking out her tongue.

'And this is for you, Will,' said Helen, passing him a white parcel with illustrated robins on it. Will took it from her with a smile. He too wanted to rip the paper from it quickly too but didn't want to ruin his cool, so he casually pulled at the Sellotape, unveiling it slowly. Inside was a white T-shirt with a red Vans logo and a black VHS tape.

'Is that the top you wanted, love?'

'Yes, thank you.' Will inspected the VHS. 'What's this?'

'It's footage from your gigs. Mick helped me put it together.'

'Well, I hope it hasn't got the last one on it,' said Will wryly.

Helen smiled sympathetically and said nothing.

'I'm kidding. That's awesome, thanks, Mum.'

Around midday, Mick arrived, wearing a thick green knitted sweater with a big brown reindeer on it. Will shook his hand, rough and huge compared to his. He hugged Helen tightly and kissed her quickly on the lips. This was the first time Will had seen any real physical contact between them and he instinctively averted his eyes.

'I hear you're enrolling on a songwriting course in London, Will?'

'Hand-picked for it,' Helen added.

Will fiddled with the woollen sleeve of his jumper. His mum had really harped on over the last few weeks about how proud she was of him for getting on the course, to the point that the expectation now made him nauseous.

'That's great, when does it start?'

'Next month.'

Mick smiled; his teeth were greyish and he shut his mouth quickly, as if conscious of them.

'Well, all the best with it.'

There was a silence. Will knew that Mick was thinking about Jake, about what his son could have achieved in music, given the chance. He test-drove some words of comfort in his head but decided nothing seemed quite right.

At the dinner table, Helen scurried around making sure everyone's drink was topped up, had enough gravy, bread sauce, potatoes and veg. She realised she'd forgotten the Christmassy napkins and was about to run back to the kitchen to retrieve them when Will rolled his eyes and told her to sit down and eat her food. Mick winked at him covertly in agreement.

After they'd finished the turkey, they pulled the Christmas crackers together – Will with Izzy, Helen with Mick. Little pieces of plastic tat fell out onto the table: a compass, a ring, a pencil sharpener and a comb. Will slid his to Izzy, who smiled toothily. Helen demanded they put the paper hats on and Will rested his on the top of his head, not pulling it down fully in minor protest.

Two Christmases had passed since Will's dad had died, both of which had been pretty bleak. It felt odd, but not altogether unpleasant, to have a fourth person at the table again. Mick, reaching for some common ground, plumped for football and regurgitated something he'd heard on the radio about Sutton being isolated now without Shearer. Will smiled and met him halfway. Helen brought in apple crumble and custard for dessert; none of them actually liked Christmas pudding and it seemed silly to stick to tradition for the sake of it.

When they had finished eating, Mick proposed a toast, firstly to the family for welcoming him in, and secondly to his Jake, who 'couldn't be here', his voice catching in the air as his name passed his lips. Will could feel his eyes filling up, powerless to stop them. He looked at Mick, who also began to weep. Helen put her hand on his as he continued to pay tribute to his son.

'I'm sorry,' said Mick, excusing himself from the table. Helen got up with him and wrapped her arms around him.

'It's OK, let it all out,' she said.

Will felt compelled to stand up too; he patted Mick on the back as he stood in his mother's arms. Izzy, not knowing where to look, pretended to scrape up one last spoonful of crumble from an empty bowl.

That evening, they muddled through a game of *Trivial Pursuit* together and watched an old episode of *Only Fools and Horses*. After Izzy had gone up to bed, Helen went to the kitchen to fix them teas. Mick took the opportunity to speak to Will directly, sitting down next to him on the couch.

'She's very special, your mum, you know that?'

Will nodded.

'And I'm serious about her.'

Will fiddled with the party hat he'd forgotten was still on his head. It had been a long day and he could feel the floaty effects of the alcohol on his brain but knew he had to say something.

'Look after her while I'm away in London, won't you?'

Mick looked at Will and held his gaze. 'I will. Promise.'

'She's not as strong as she makes out,' said Will quietly.

Mick smiled, a laboured, uneven smile, one he cut short as Helen returned with a precariously balanced tray of tea and mince pies.

'So, shall we watch the video then?' she asked.

'Sure,' said Will, turning to look at Mick again. 'If that's OK with you?'

'Of course,' he said softly.

Helen sat herself down on the couch and put her head on Mick's shoulder. Will slid the video out of its case, crawled across the carpet on his knees and pushed it into the player.

It began with some shaky footage from their first gig. The songs were loose and underdeveloped, the camcorder audio tinny and muffled. He turned his head and saw Mick watching on, beaming with pride, Helen stroking his brawny arm. The tape then cut sharply to the Battle of the Bands that they had won. Jake moved gracefully across the stage, twirling the microphone around by its lead. He climbed up on the drum riser and bellowed out the chorus with one arm aloft, before moving to the other side of the stage and ruffling Will's hair as he played the solo. His movements were theatrical and mesmerising, and Will realised that no one had ever been watching him on stage – they wouldn't have been able to take their eyes off of Jake.

Well, no one except Amy, that is.

CHAPTER 36

Will sat slumped on the sofa, finishing a plate of stringy cold cuts. He took the last swig of a stubby and placed it down on the coffee table. It was Boxing Day, late afternoon. He flicked though the television channels, watched a few minutes of *Jumanji* before turning it off. The blank screen was feathered with dust; he stared at it for a few seconds, levered himself off the couch and headed upstairs.

Luke and Pete both had family plans, and he'd not heard from Amy. So, feeling at a loose end, he decided to head out. He didn't tell his mum he was going out; she would suggest that they all went for a walk together – one of those status-defining festive walks she'd seen middle-class families do – and he just wanted to be alone. He'd spent a lot of time alone over the last few months; it had become his default setting, the one at which he felt most at home. He pulled his green parka on and snuck out the back door, pausing to pet Elmo on the driveway, his coat shiny and cold.

He strolled past the little parade of shops and through the park towards town. Darkness was beginning to fall and the streets were eerily empty. He approached the café. Chloe had drawn the short straw and was just closing up for the day.

'Merry Christmas,' Will called from across the street.

Chloe, struggling with the shutters, gestured him over. Will crossed the street and gave her a hand, holding the cold iron sheet down as she locked them in place.

'Merry Christmas.' Chloe smiled, giving him a warm but self-conscious hug.

Will, buoyed by the encounter, continued towards the square and poked his head into Tony's. Tony was cashing up but welcomed him in, Spiritualized spinning away over the speakers.

'I wasn't sure you'd be open today.'

'Yeah, just for the afternoon – a lot of people with vouchers and kids exchanging the shite their parents got them.' He laughed.

'I got you something.'

Will reached into a carrier bag and handed him a four-pack of ales.

'Thank you. You needn't have, though.'

Will smiled warmly. 'I wanted to. You took a chance on us. I'll never forget that.'

Tony inspected the label on the bottles, German and strong. 'You guys deserved it.'

Will shuffled uncomfortably on the spot. 'I'm off to London in the new year, but I'll come say hello whenever I'm back.'

'You better.' Tony smiled.

Will surprised himself by giving him a big hug.

'Take care,' said Tony, gently tapping his back.

Will exited the store, back out into the bitter cold.

'SharpShooter forever,' shouted Tony on his way out.

*

Amy lay on top of her thick winter duvet, head propped up with a pillow. Her door was shut, but she could hear echoes of her parents arguing about something trivial downstairs. She'd always hated Boxing Day – the literal cold turkey come-down from Christmas. Both sets of grandparents had come over for Christmas Day and the house now seemed so quiet and empty. Charlotte was away with her family. They'd spoken at length on the phone and promised to spend New Year's Eve together, but for now Amy found herself alone. She flicked through the bumper issue of the *Radio Times*, but nothing piqued her interest. She pulled on her winter coat, wrapped a burgundy scarf tightly around her neck and headed out. Her glittery-black Converse struggled for traction on the icy pavement as she headed towards the town.

Will crossed the park; a small boy playing with his shiny new remote-control car lost control and smashed it into the foot of the bench. He walked towards The Griffin, deciding to pop in for one. The windows were steamy, but he could tell from the blurry moving shapes that it was busy inside. Through the glass he could hear the jukebox churning out Slade, a day late. He pushed open the door and surveyed a group of guys in fleeces and chinos by the door – he fancied a drink but couldn't stomach an awkward catch-up with anyone from school. Satisfied that the coast was clear, he sidled up to the bar and ordered a JD and Coke, handing over the crisp £20 note his nan had put in his Christmas card. As he received his change, he turned his head to the right, scanning for a free table, and saw a girl with dark hair walking purposefully away from the bar with her drink.

It's Amy. He was sure of it.

It was only the back of her head, but the way she carried herself, the clothes she wore, he knew instantly it was her. A peculiar feeling hit his chest – a flurry of emotions he couldn't immediately identify. He thought that if this was a scene in a film, he would tap her on the shoulder and a girl who looked nothing like Amy would turn around. But it was her all right.

'Amy,' he called out, his voice weaker than he expected. She turned around slowly, swept her hair out of her eyes and smiled.

'Will Green, drinking alone. I thought I'd never see the day.'

Will took in her face, sleek and beguiling.

'I could say the same to you. What are you doing here?'

'I had to get out of the house, my parents were driving me mad,' replied Amy, making a gun to her head with her fingers.

Will gripped his icy drink tightly, making his already cold hands colder. 'Mind if I join you?' he asked.

Amy took a sip of her drink. 'Are you sure you want to?'

'Of course. Why wouldn't I?' said Will, perplexed.

'Well, I left you a message saying I would be home for Christmas if you wanted to meet up, and you didn't call.'

Will stood there frozen. *Piece of shit machine.* 'I'm sorry, I didn't get it. Answerphone's playing up.'

239

Amy laughed scornfully. 'If you didn't want to see me it's fine, no need to blame the machine.'

'Of course I wanted to see you. I've not thought of much else these last few months, to be honest,' he said, his face rippling with red.

They sat down at a table in the corner by the fireplace. Amy opened a packet of cigarettes.

'Want one?' she asked, her powder-blue eyes still knocking Will back.

'I don't smoke.'

'Neither do I.' She smiled, lighting it.

'I heard your song on the radio.'

'Oh, really?'

'It made me cry.'

Will looked away. 'I'm sorry.'

'No. In a good way.' She took a drag of her cigarette and exhaled a small cloud of grey smoke. 'Was it about me?

Will fidgeted in his seat. 'No, it was about Jake.'

'That's a relief.'

'You did ask me never to write a song about you.'

'I remember,' said Amy.

They both laughed and held on to each other's gaze for a moment, until one of them looked away – an unspoken game of chicken.

Will took a sip of his drink. 'Are you seeing anyone in London?'

'I was. But it was never going to work out,' replied Amy, rubbing her brow with her hand.

'How come?'

'I'm not sure I can say.'

'Go on. You can tell me,' said Will, moving in closer.

'He was my lecturer. It got messy.'

Will stifled a laugh. 'Oh my god!'

Amy ignored his reaction. 'How about you? Still batting off the groupies, I'm sure.'

'Ha, hardly.' Will shrugged.

He looked at her again, braver this time. 'How did it come to this, Amy?'

'How do you mean?'

'Us.'

'There is no *us*,' said Amy, stubbing out her cigarette in the glass ashtray.

'Exactly. But I still can't get my head around why.'

Will stirred the ice in his drink with the straw. 'Do you still think about me at all?'

Amy said nothing, keeping her face perfectly still, as if the tiniest of movements would count as an answer. 'Where are you heading next?' she asked.

'No idea.'

'Let's walk. Together… like we used to.'

They knocked back the remains of their drinks and left the pub. It was beginning to snow now, tiny white flecks that spiralled down and refused to settle. They headed in the direction of the town. Amy pulled her hood up to shield herself from the wind. Will held out his arm and she linked hers inside it to stop herself sliding on the ice. They stopped in the park, sitting down on adjacent swings, rocking backwards and forwards, finding it easier to talk when they weren't facing each other.

'What's the plan, Will?'

'How d'you mean?'

'For you.'

Will cleared his throat, glad to now have an answer to that question. 'I've been invited to join a songwriting course in London.'

'That's amazing!' Amy turned to look at him, his nose flush from the cold and his teeth chattering an irregular rhythm. 'I'm proud of you.'

Will turned his head to face hers, the buzzing in his ears now a low drone. 'Christ, I've missed you, Amy. More than you could know.'

She leant her head over towards his, stopping a few centimetres away from his lips. 'I've missed you too.'

They looked at each other for a moment and kissed clumsily, as if making up for lost time. Her lips were cold and tender, her mouth wet and familiar, as he cradled her head with his hand.

'Was that OK?' he asked.

Amy pulled down her hood, revealing her face fully again. 'Yes.'

They kissed again, longer this time. Will offered out his hand and helped Amy up from the swings. She continued to hold it as they walked past the frozen pond, back towards the main road.

'Where will you be staying in London?' she asked.

'I don't know yet. I need to sort something out.'

Amy looked at him and smiled. 'It's OK. I think I might know a place.'

ACKNOWLEDGEMENTS

Having played guitar in bands for much of my adult life, I'd always felt like I wanted to write a music-based novel. I hoped to capture the real highs and lows of being in a band plugging away on the 'toilet-circuit.' But more generally, I hoped to capture those teenage years when anything seemed possible, when the summers were a mix of joy and confusion, and doomed first-love beckoned.

When the pandemic hit in 2020, life slowed down sufficiently for me to finally start work on it. Foolishly, I underestimated just how much work writing a novel involves! For that reason, I am grateful to my friends and family for all their words of support and the encouragement I needed to keep going. I am also extremely grateful to my partner Liz for putting up with endless evenings of me tapping away on my laptop.

Thank you also to Anna Jean Hughes, who gave me hugely valuable feedback on the first draft and helped shape the second one massively, and to my good friend

Michael Winder whose scribbled notes contained valuable insight.

A big thank you to everyone at The Book Guild for seeing something in this tale and helping it to see the light of day. Through the late nights and the coffee-fuelled early mornings, it was a pleasure to feel the story take shape and I hope you all enjoy hanging out with the characters as much as I did.

Richard Williams, August 2022

For writing and publishing news, or
recommendations of new titles to read,
sign up to the Book Guild newsletter:

SCAN ME